HELLBOY
ANIMATED
THE BLACK WEDDING

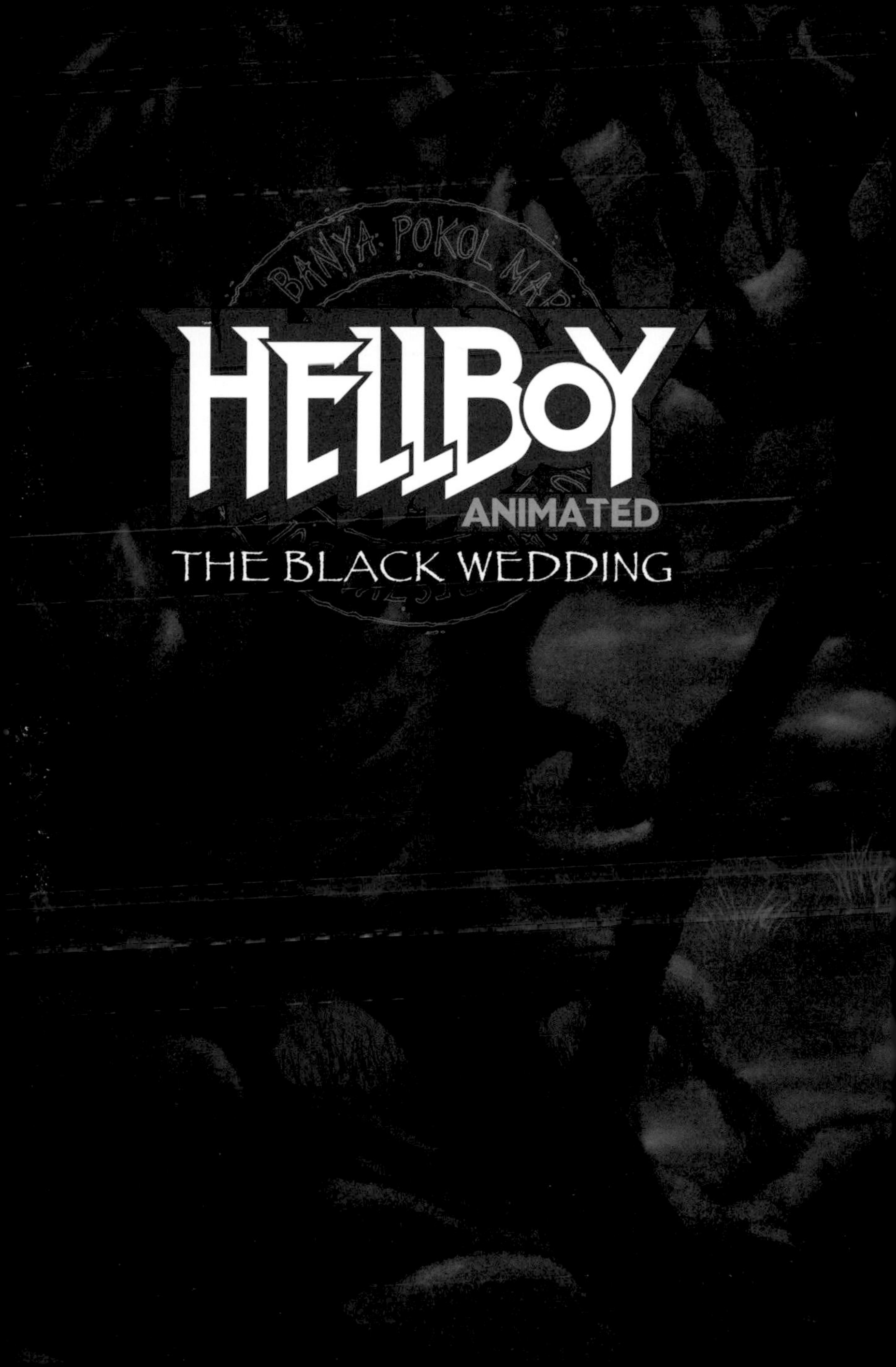

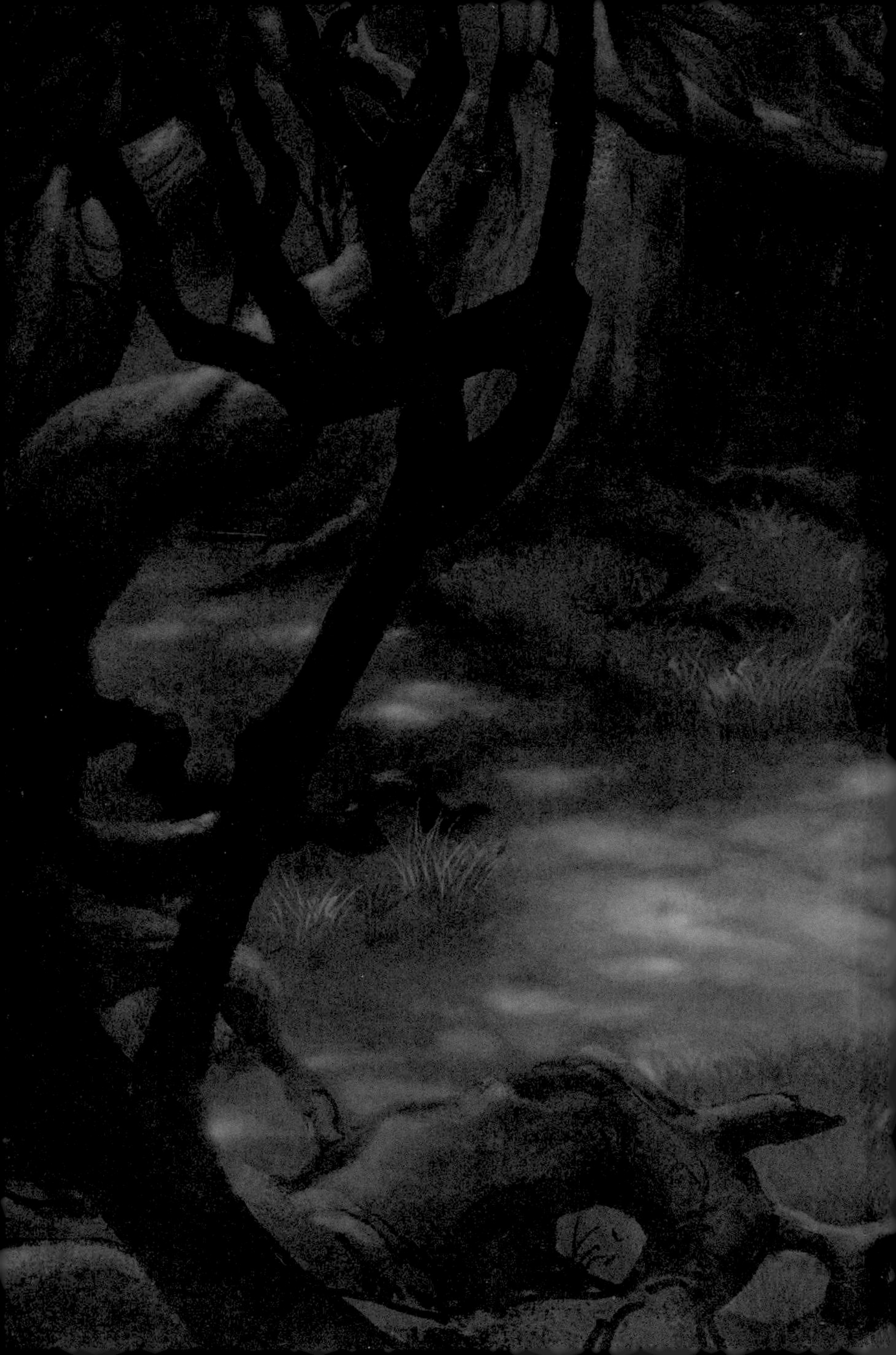

HELLBOY
ANIMATED

THE BLACK WEDDING

Story by JIM PASCOE

Art by RICK LACY

Colors by DAN JACKSON

Letters by BLAMBOT'S NATE PIEKOS

PINUP

Art by MIKE MIGNOLA

Colors by DAVE STEWART

PYRAMID OF DEATH

Story by TAD STONES

Art by FABIO LAGUNA

Colors by MICHELLE MADSEN

Letters by BLAMBOT'S NATE PIEKOS

Cover by JEFF MATSUDA

Cover Colors by ARON LUSEN

Hellboy and the B.P.R.D. created by MIKE MIGNOLA

Dark Horse Books™

Publisher MIKE RICHARDSON

Editors SCOTT ALLIE & MATT DRYER

Assistant Editor RACHEL EDIDIN

Art Director CARY GRAZZINI

Designer KEITH WOOD

Special Thanks to MIKE and CHRISTINE MIGNOLA,
DAVE STEWART, GUY DAVIS, JOHN ARCUDI, TAD STONES,
JASON HVAM, and DAN JACKSON

Published by
Dark Horse Books
A division of Dark Horse Comics, Inc.
10956 SE Main Street
Milwaukie, OR 97222

darkhorse.com

To find a comics shop in your area,
call the Comic Shop Locator Service toll-free at 1-888-266-4226

First Edition: January 2007
ISBN-10: 1-59307-700-9
ISBN-13: 978-1-59307-700-6

1 3 5 7 9 10 8 6 4 2

Printed in the United States of America

Approximately eleven years ago, I stood in the office of a Walt Disney Television executive and pitched *Hellboy: the Animated Series*. This scenario wasn't as crazy as it sounds, because this guy had stressed that Disney was looking for something different, something *edgy* for prime time. Besides, the time seemed right. Bruce Timm had rocked the animation world with a version of Batman that showed American animation capable of more than preteen morality lessons. Elsewhere, Mulder and Scully were at the peak of their paranormal investigating popularity. So there I was, pitching Hellboy as an animated *X Files*, knowing it could be a lot more.

As I recall, the executive responded with something like, "I love it, *but…*" which is the response pitches get in Hollywood ninety-nine out of ninety-nine-and-a-half times. He gave lots of reasons for passing on it—good ones too—but I always felt that it boiled down to "It doesn't feel like *The Simpsons*."

Let us now pause and give thanks to Matt Groening and company for being so unique and successful that they blinded all television executives to other possibilities of animation. They may have saved us from "Heckboy" and the sight of Mike Mignola's creations riding down Disneyland's Main Street with Donald Duck and Cinderella. "Look Momma, I wanna picture with Rasputin!"

Years later, I started production on a TV spinoff of Disney's *Atlantis: The Lost Empire*. It starred a team of adventurers who explored arcane secrets and forgotten cities and fought bizarre or mystical creatures. I thought it might be the closest I would ever get to Hellboy and wasted no time in hiring Mike Mignola to help, as he had with the feature film. He was surprised at how dark some of our early scripts were: "Will they let you do this?"

Turned out, no. They wouldn't.

So there went my collaboration with Mike. A few years later, the Mouse and I parted ways. Meanwhile, Guillermo del Toro was in preproduction on his Hellboy movie and spent a lot of time talking about how an animated series should follow it. Guillermo is a hard man to ignore and, as busy as he was, kept pushing until his studio felt obliged to take note. Slowly, a couple of corporations, a network, two film studios, and a squad of agents and lawyers began their Byzantine dance that featured false starts, a deal immolation, and the phoenix-like resurrection of the animated Hellboy project as a series of DVD movies. This brings us to the strange creation you hold in your hand, a comic based on a cartoon based on a comic, an alternate universe of Hellboy.

It was part of the deal that the animated Hellboy not be drawn like Mike Mignola's Hellboy. I'm sure there are all sorts of licensing and merchandising reasons for that, but the only thing that mattered to me was that it was Mike's wish, too. When you see the Mignola version on the cover of a comic, you're getting canon, you're getting Hellboy walking in the shadowy world of Mike's creation. The stories in those comics will continue to paint the epic mural of Hellboy's life, and possibly the end of the world. I mean, you know what that right hand is for, don't you?

So what are *these* comics? These are tales from the world of *Hellboy Animated*, a universe whose general structure was laid out when Mike and I co-wrote the stories for the first two DVDs. The characters' relationships and the major beats of Hellboy's life are the same here as those of the original, but the details have mutated. Hellboy has not been labeled Beast of the Apocalypse yet, Professor Broom is still alive, the B.P.R.D. headquarters has already moved into its mountain stronghold, and Lobster Johnson is… maybe I'll leave *some* secrets to be discovered in animation.

These are new missions for Hellboy, stand-alone adventures of the world's greatest paranormal investigator and his colleagues. Above all else, they're meant to be fun and perhaps come closest to that original "animated *X Files*" pitch. Mike and I give notes to keep things from conflicting from what we want to do in future movies, while Scott Allie and Matt Dryer make sure the stuff ends up in a form that works on the page. You'll also find a lighthearted back-up story of Hellboy's early years on the Air Force base when he was a maniac fanboy, decades before they took over the media.

I am thankful for Mike's continued involvement in *Hellboy Animated* and am continuously impressed with the quality of ideas that stream out of his head, seemingly at light speed. It is all so exciting that, in many ways, I feel my career is just starting. So here I sit at my desk, surrounded by the model sheets, storyboards, and scripts of a dream I had eleven years ago. Life is pretty good, and the fact that down the hall there's a huge staff of artists animating *The Simpsons* makes it all the sweeter.

Tad Stones
Burbank, CA
August 3, 2006

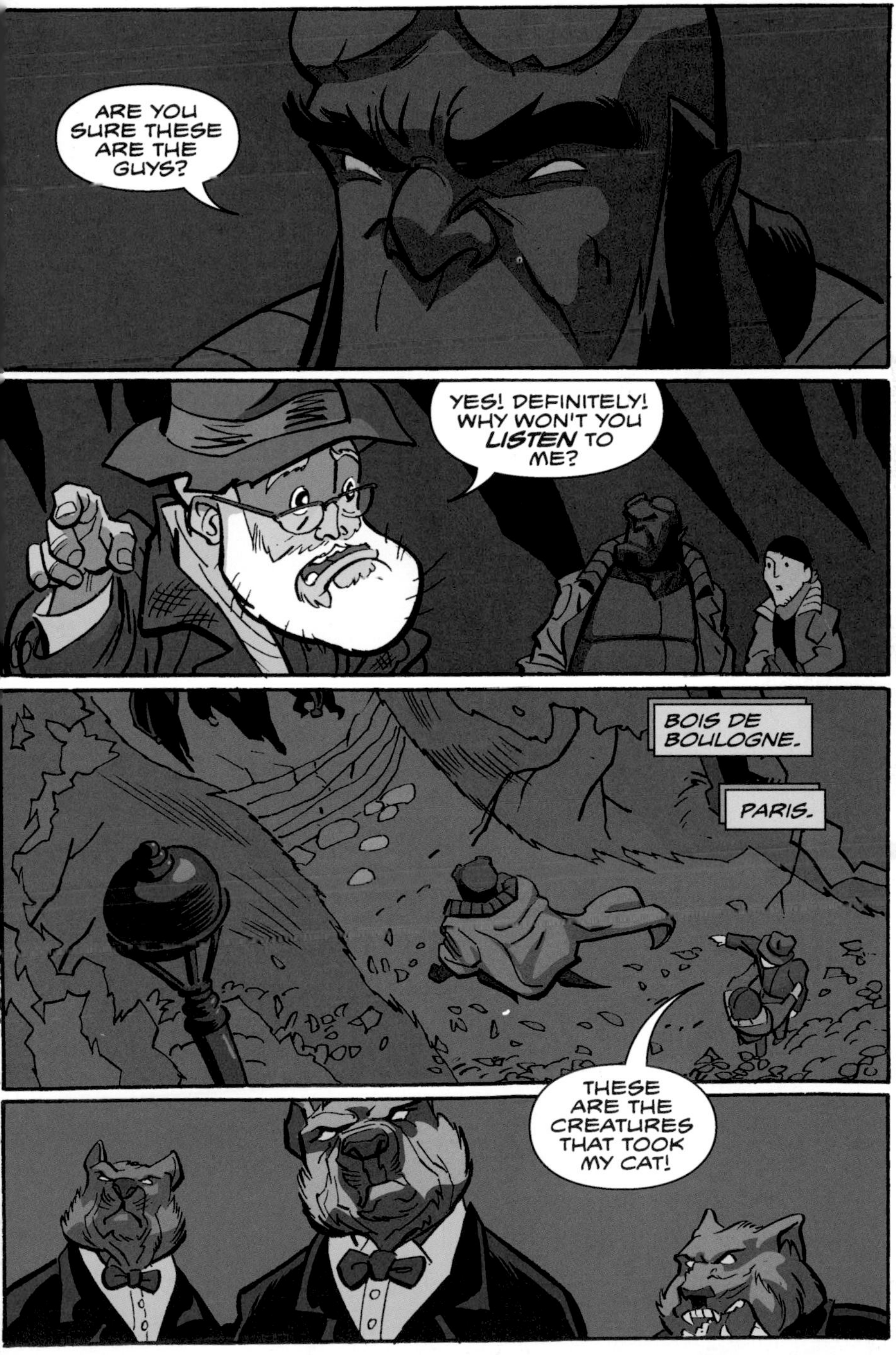
ARE YOU SURE THESE ARE THE GUYS?
YES! DEFINITELY! WHY WON'T YOU *LISTEN* TO ME?
BOIS DE BOULOGNE.
PARIS.
THESE ARE THE CREATURES THAT TOOK MY CAT!

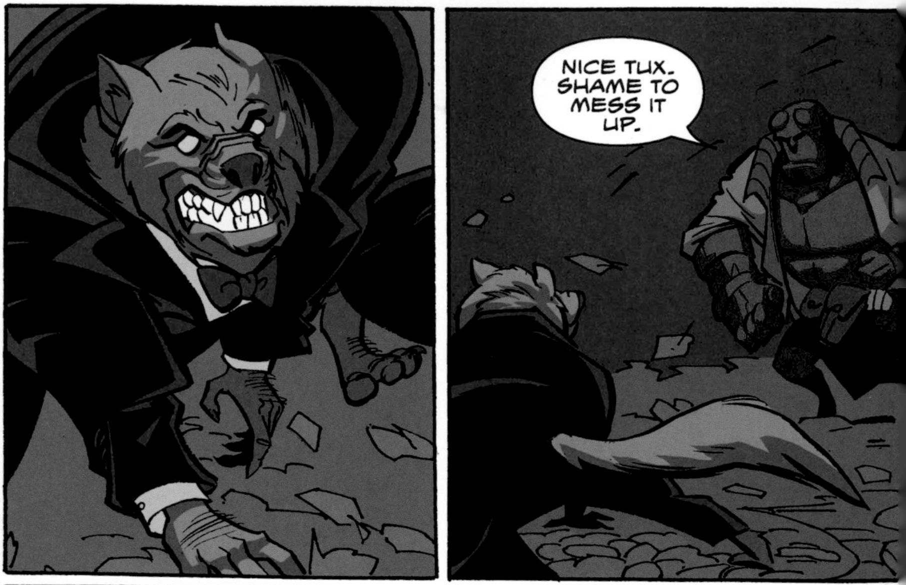
NICE TUX. SHAME TO MESS IT UP.

THE BLACK WEDDING

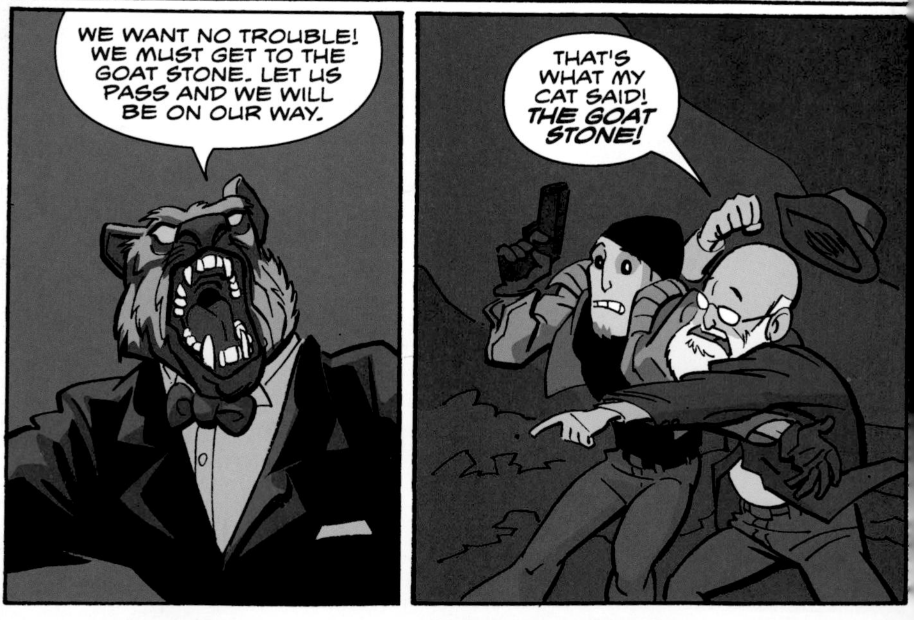
WE WANT NO TROUBLE! WE MUST GET TO THE GOAT STONE. LET US PASS AND WE WILL BE ON OUR WAY.
THAT'S WHAT MY CAT SAID! *THE GOAT STONE!*

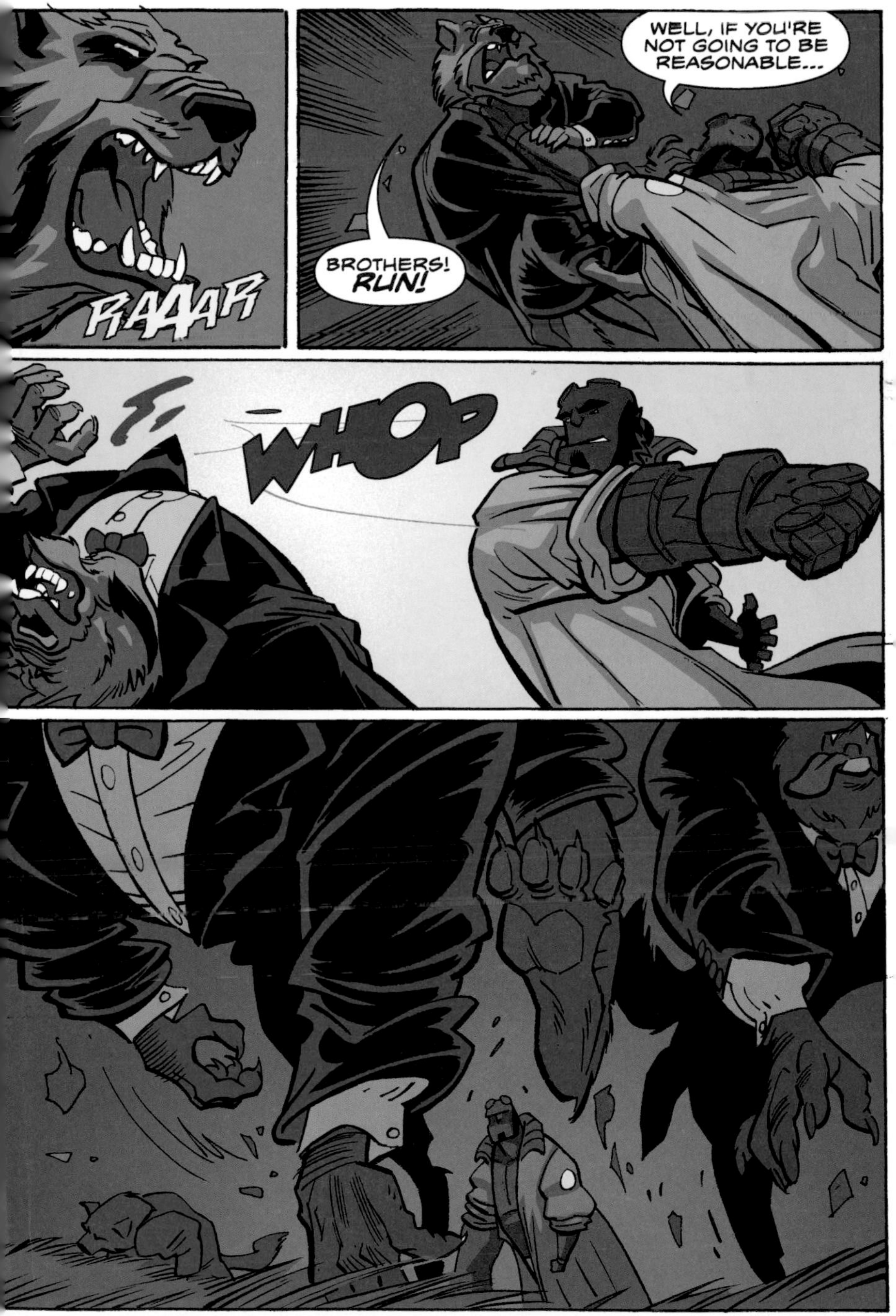
RAAAR
WELL, IF YOU'RE NOT GOING TO BE REASONABLE...
BROTHERS! RUN!
WHOP

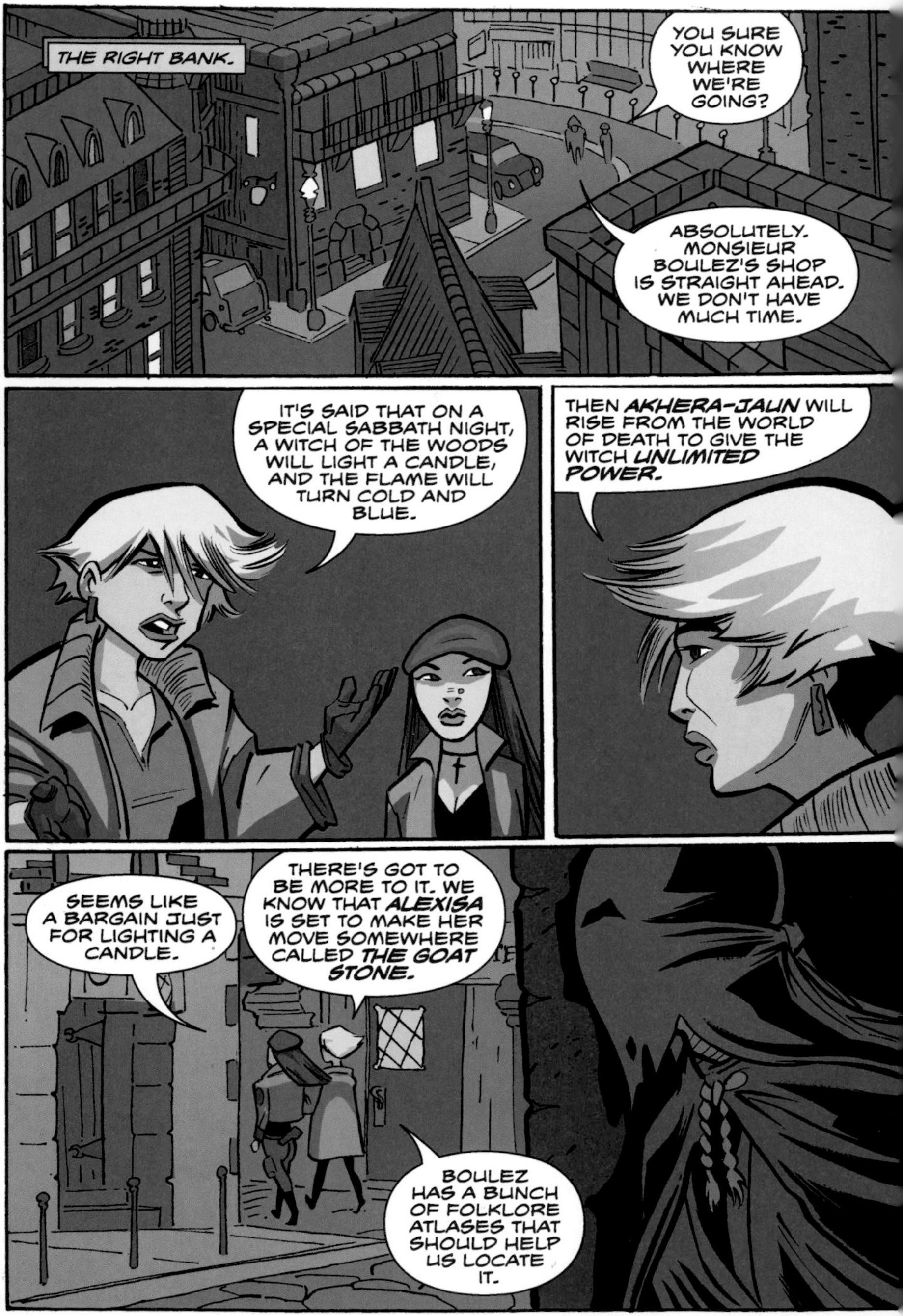
THE RIGHT BANK.
YOU SURE YOU KNOW WHERE WE'RE GOING?
ABSOLUTELY. MONSIEUR BOULEZ'S SHOP IS STRAIGHT AHEAD. WE DON'T HAVE MUCH TIME.
IT'S SAID THAT ON A SPECIAL SABBATH NIGHT, A WITCH OF THE WOODS WILL LIGHT A CANDLE, AND THE FLAME WILL TURN COLD AND BLUE.
THEN AKHERA-JAUN WILL RISE FROM THE WORLD OF DEATH TO GIVE THE WITCH UNLIMITED POWER.
SEEMS LIKE A BARGAIN JUST FOR LIGHTING A CANDLE.
THERE'S GOT TO BE MORE TO IT. WE KNOW THAT ALEXISA IS SET TO MAKE HER MOVE SOMEWHERE CALLED THE GOAT STONE.
BOULEZ HAS A BUNCH OF FOLKLORE ATLASES THAT SHOULD HELP US LOCATE IT.

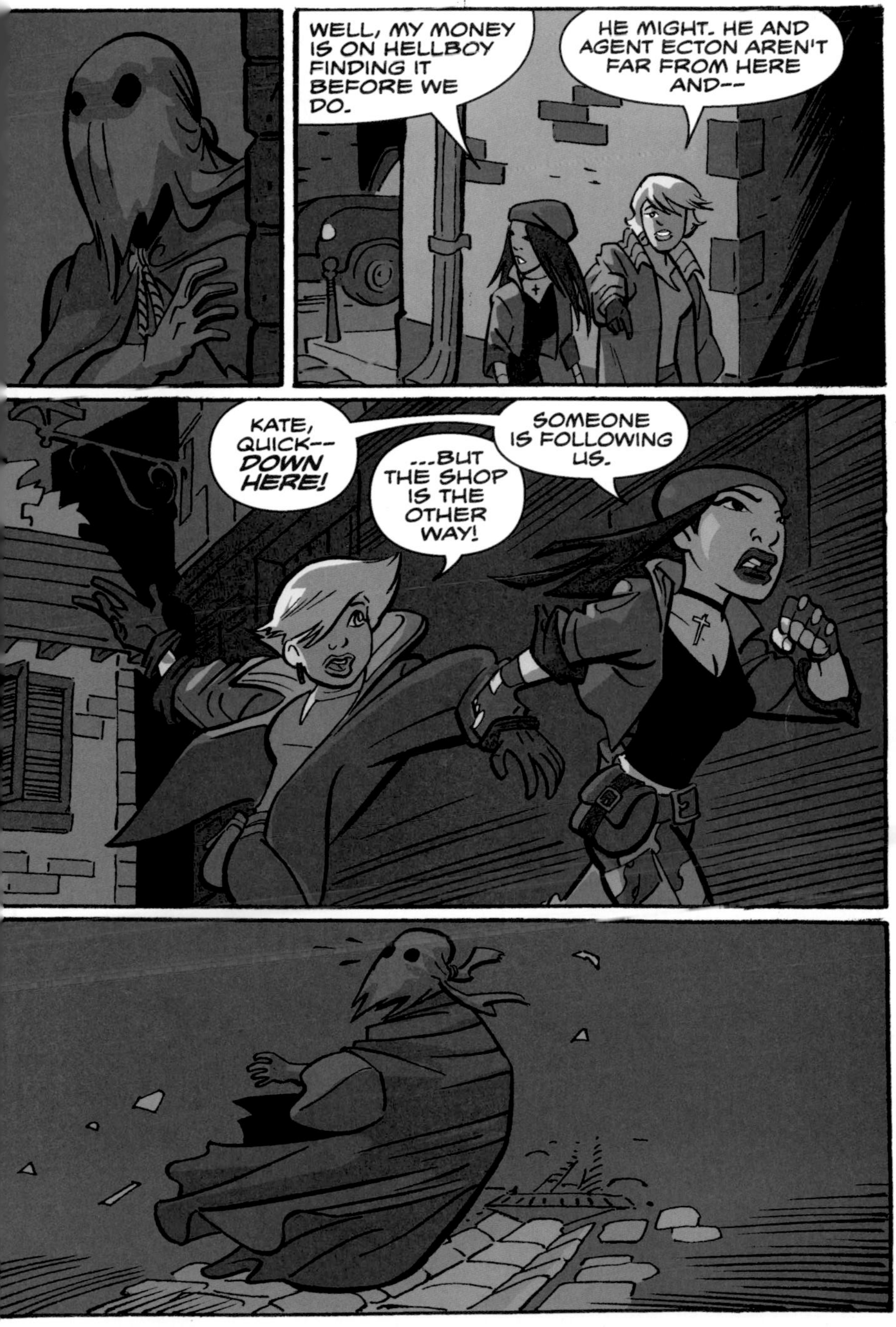
WELL, MY MONEY IS ON HELLBOY FINDING IT BEFORE WE DO.
HE MIGHT. HE AND AGENT ECTON AREN'T FAR FROM HERE AND--
SOMEONE IS FOLLOWING US.
KATE, QUICK-- DOWN HERE!
...BUT THE SHOP IS THE OTHER WAY!

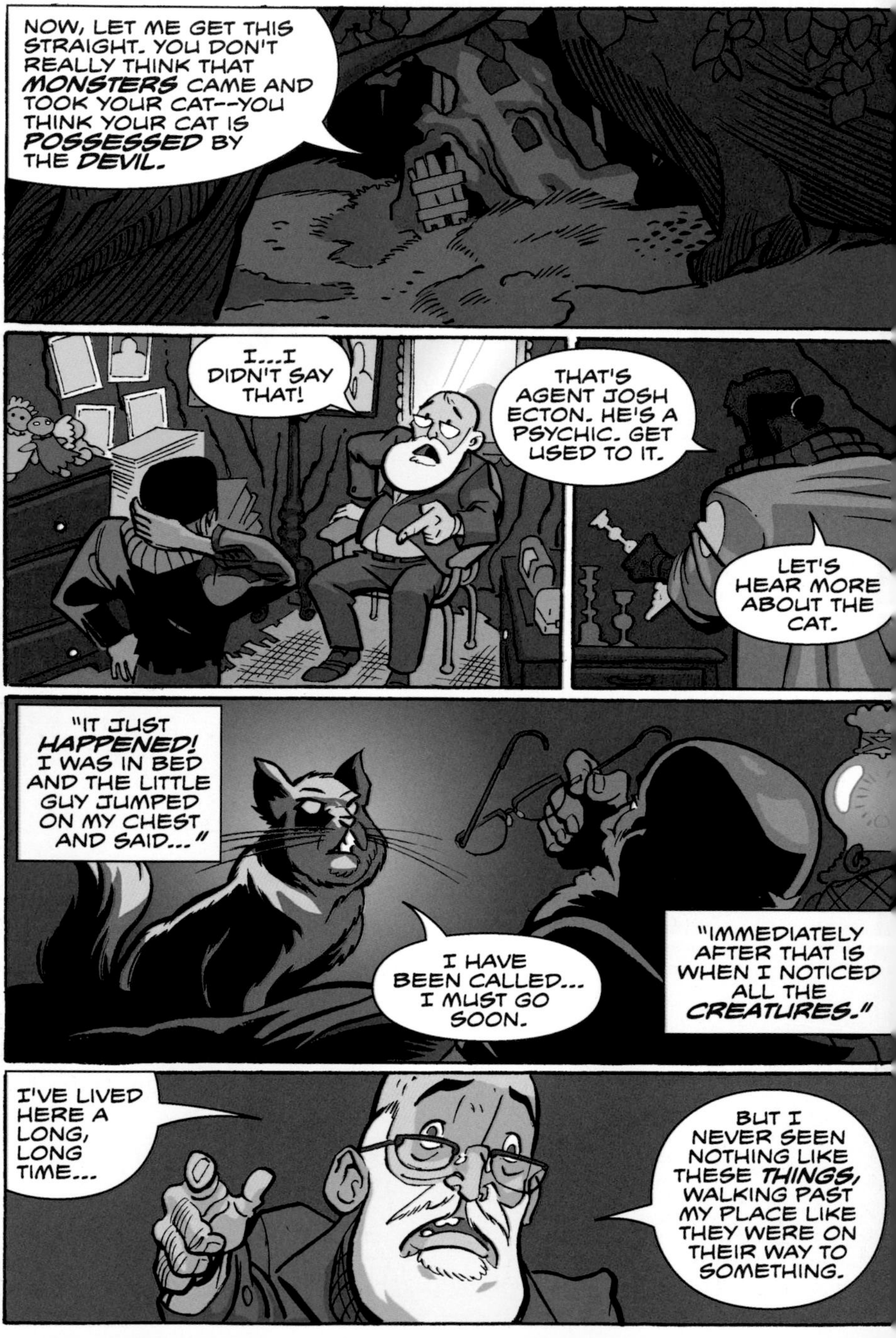
NOW, LET ME GET THIS STRAIGHT. YOU DON'T REALLY THINK THAT MONSTERS CAME AND TOOK YOUR CAT--YOU THINK YOUR CAT IS POSSESSED BY THE DEVIL.
I...I DIDN'T SAY THAT!
THAT'S AGENT JOSH ECTON. HE'S A PSYCHIC. GET USED TO IT.
LET'S HEAR MORE ABOUT THE CAT.
"IT JUST HAPPENED! I WAS IN BED AND THE LITTLE GUY JUMPED ON MY CHEST AND SAID..."
I HAVE BEEN CALLED... I MUST GO SOON.
"IMMEDIATELY AFTER THAT IS WHEN I NOTICED ALL THE CREATURES."
I'VE LIVED HERE A LONG, LONG TIME...
BUT I NEVER SEEN NOTHING LIKE THESE THINGS, WALKING PAST MY PLACE LIKE THEY WERE ON THEIR WAY TO SOMETHING.

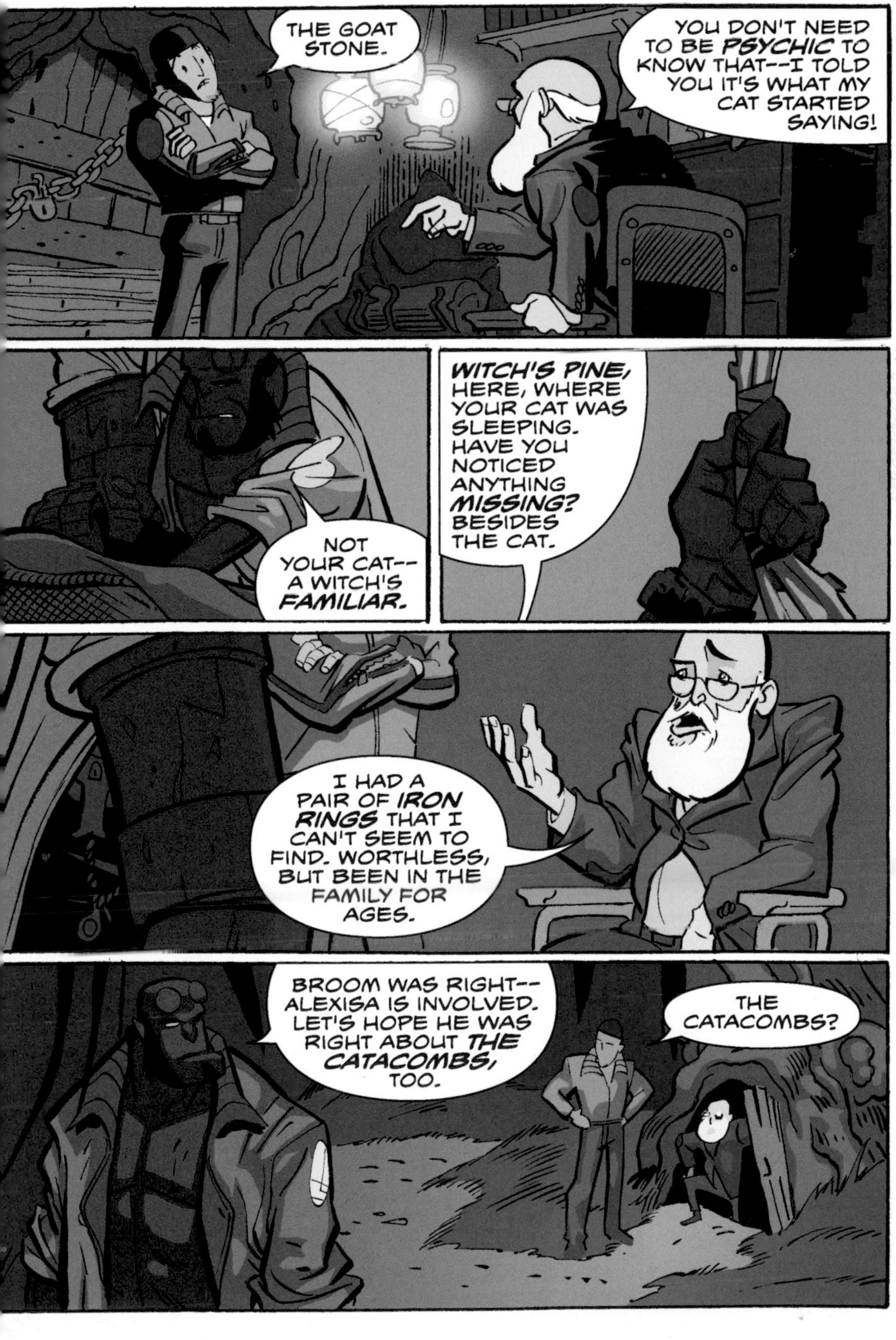
THE GOAT STONE.
YOU DON'T NEED TO BE PSYCHIC TO KNOW THAT--I TOLD YOU IT'S WHAT MY CAT STARTED SAYING!
NOT YOUR CAT-- A WITCH'S FAMILIAR.
WITCH'S PINE, HERE, WHERE YOUR CAT WAS SLEEPING. HAVE YOU NOTICED ANYTHING MISSING? BESIDES THE CAT.
I HAD A PAIR OF IRON RINGS THAT I CAN'T SEEM TO FIND. WORTHLESS, BUT BEEN IN THE FAMILY FOR AGES.
BROOM WAS RIGHT-- ALEXISA IS INVOLVED. LET'S HOPE HE WAS RIGHT ABOUT THE CATACOMBS, TOO.
THE CATACOMBS?

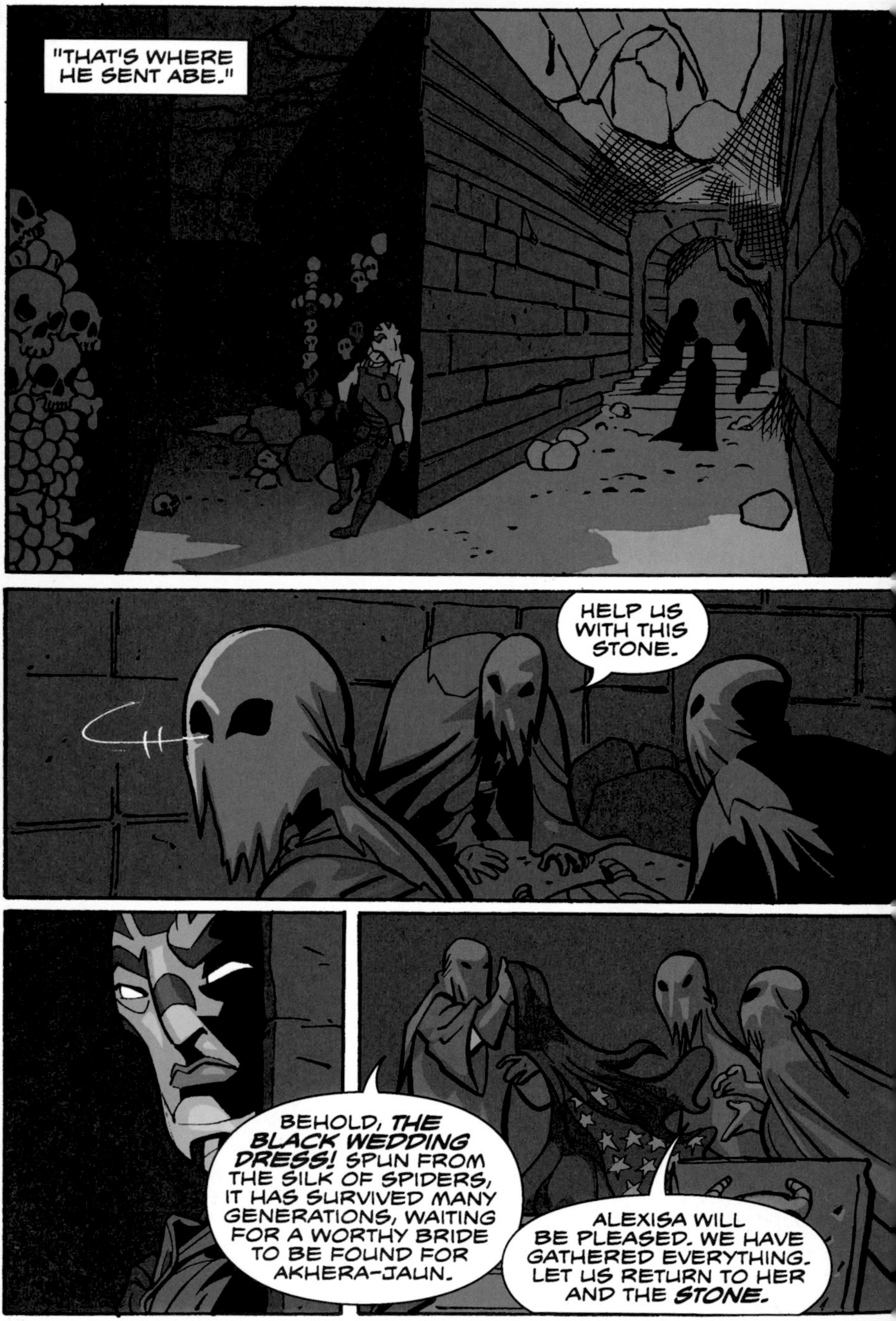
"THAT'S WHERE HE SENT ABE."
HELP US WITH THIS STONE.
BEHOLD, *THE BLACK WEDDING DRESS!* SPUN FROM THE SILK OF SPIDERS, IT HAS SURVIVED MANY GENERATIONS, WAITING FOR A WORTHY BRIDE TO BE FOUND FOR AKHERA-JAUN.
ALEXISA WILL BE PLEASED. WE HAVE GATHERED EVERYTHING. LET US RETURN TO HER AND THE *STONE.*

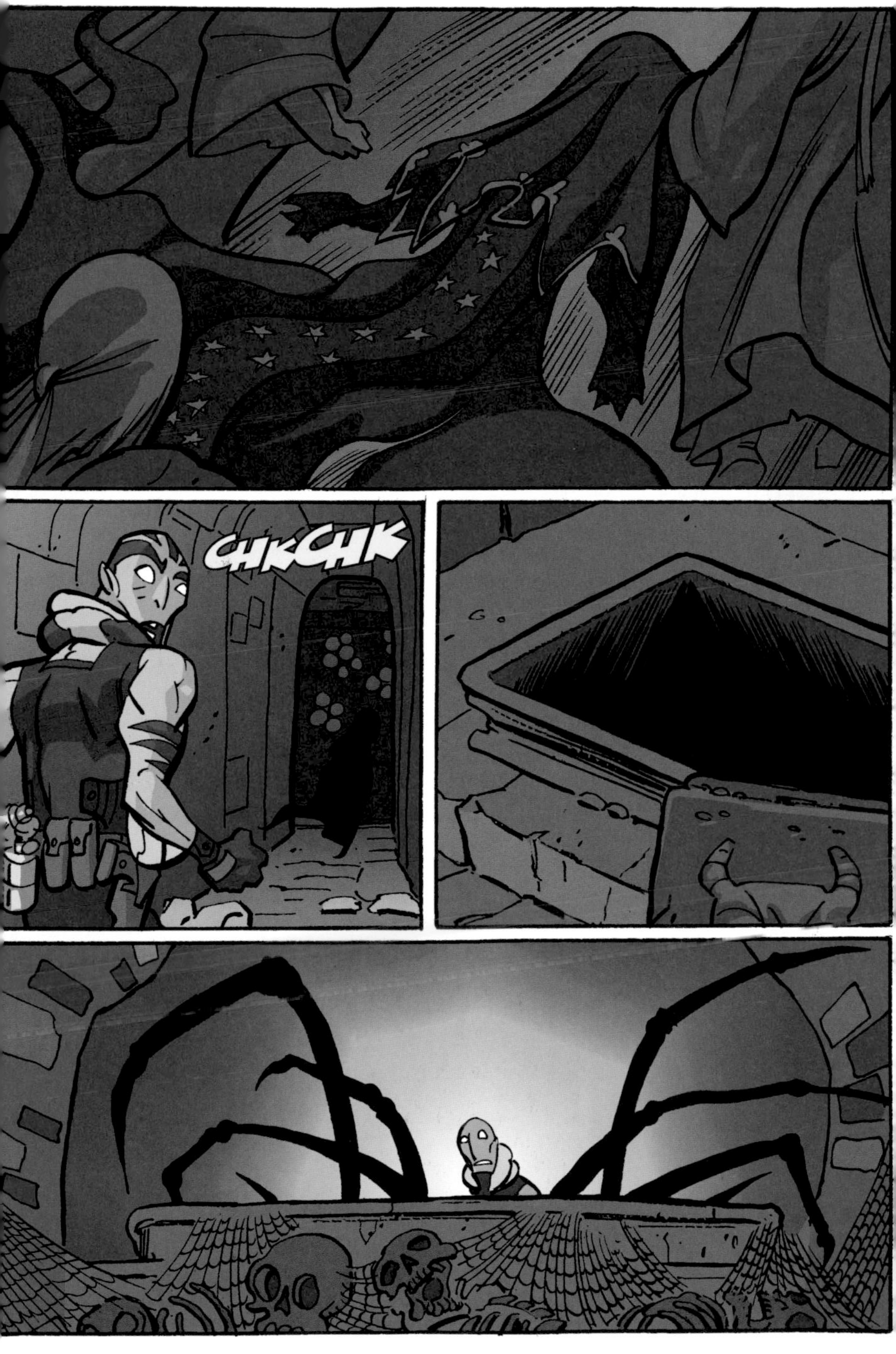
CHKCHK

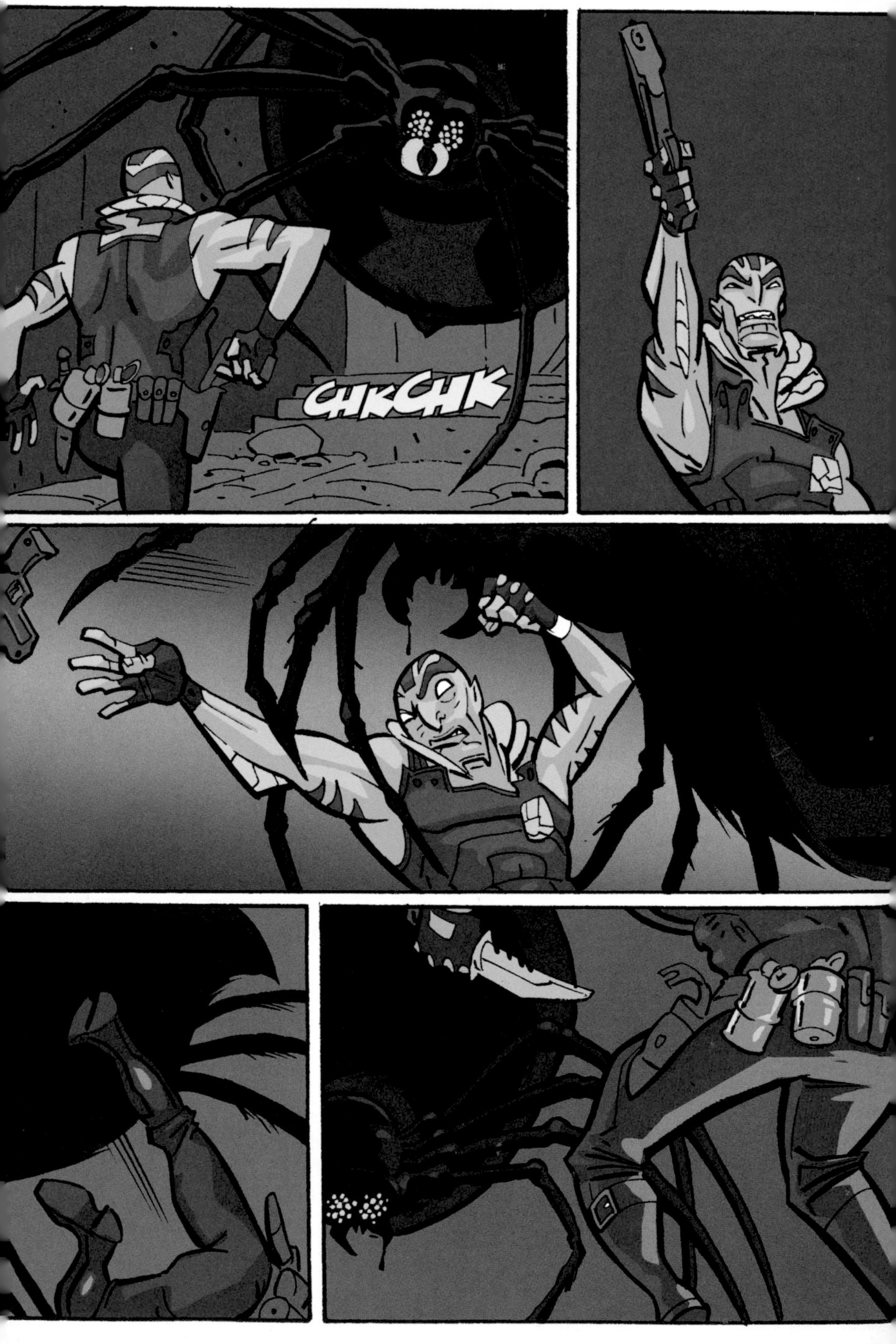
CHKCHK

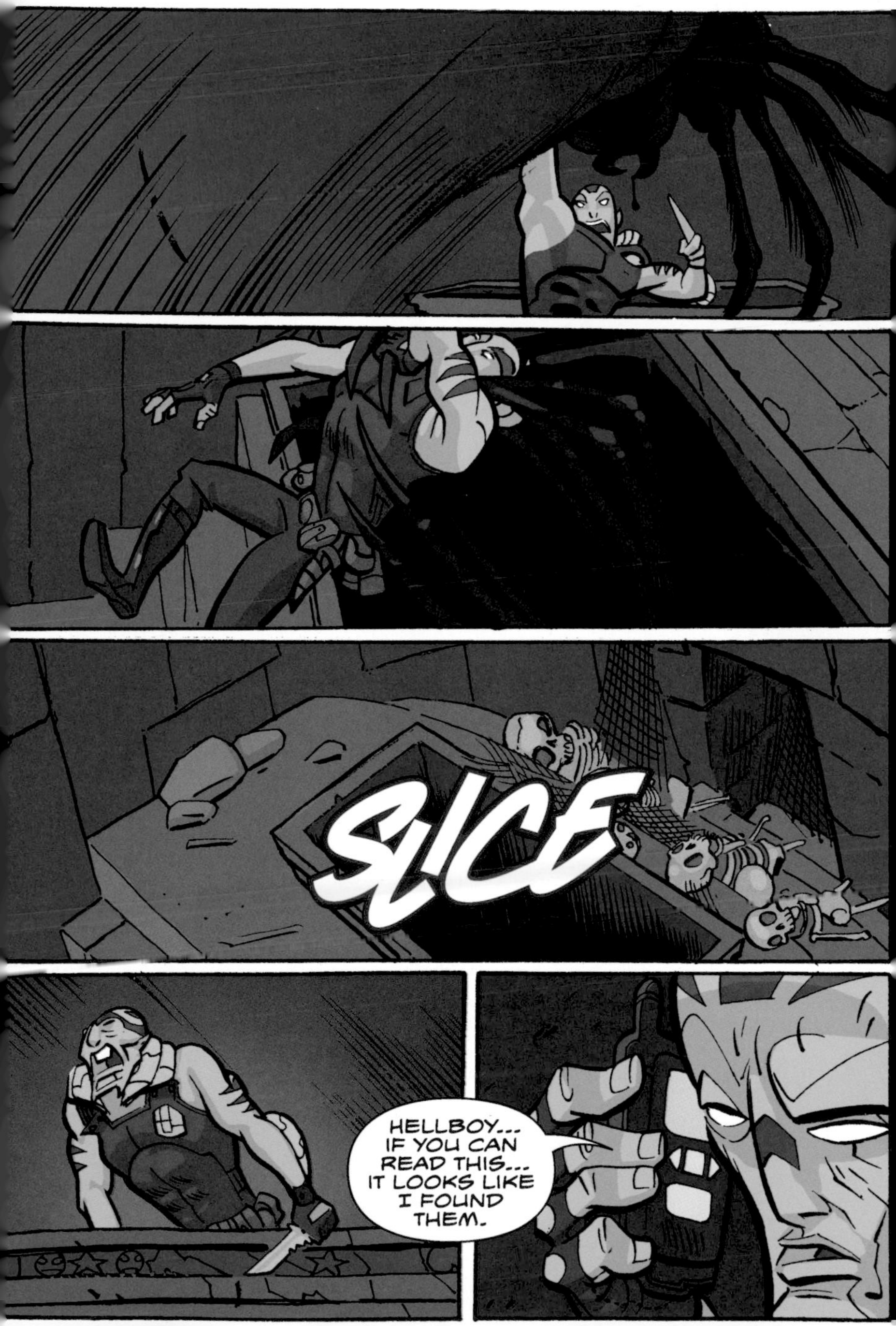
SLICE
HELLBOY... IF YOU CAN READ THIS... IT LOOKS LIKE I FOUND THEM.

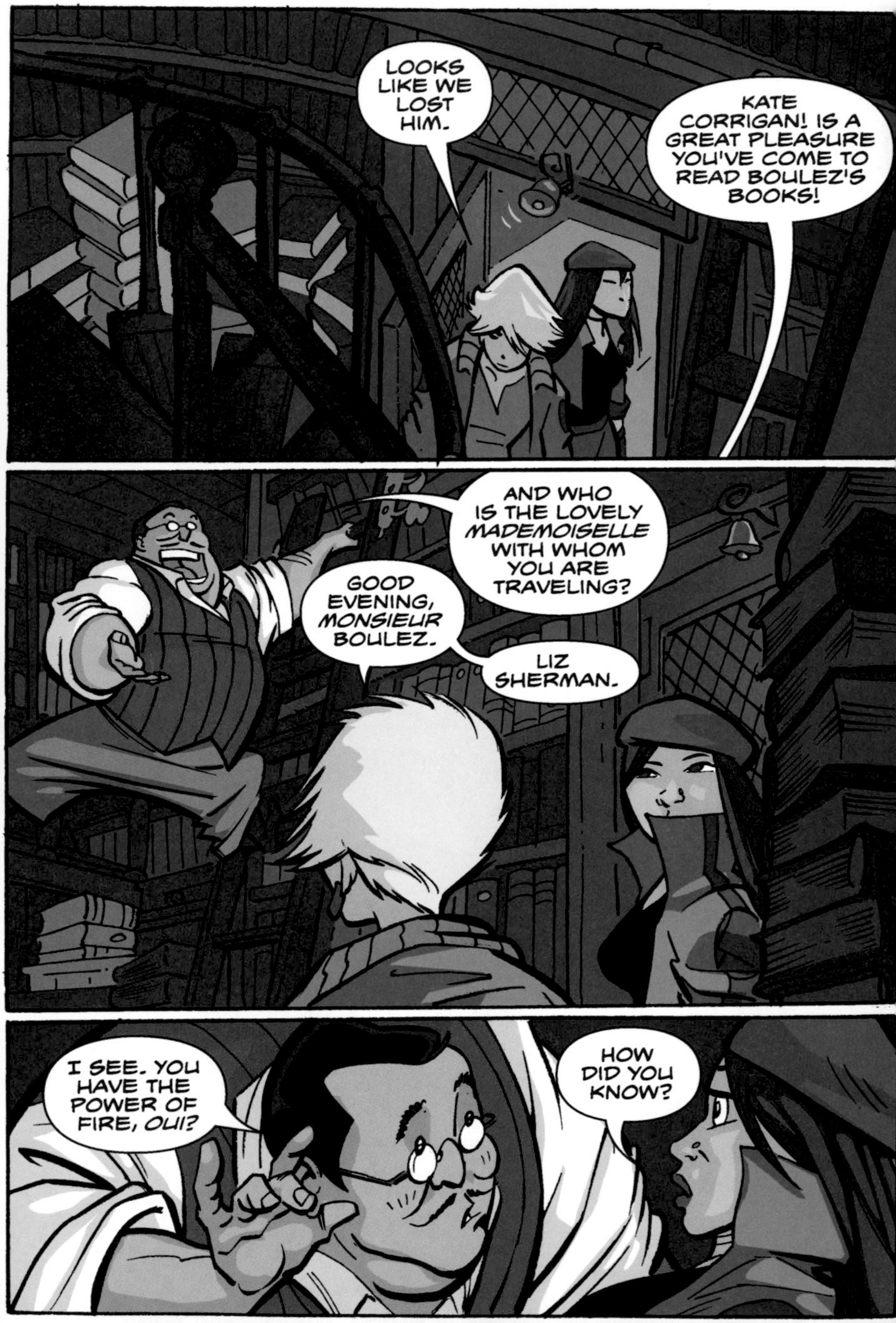
LOOKS LIKE WE LOST HIM.
KATE CORRIGAN! IS A GREAT PLEASURE YOU'VE COME TO READ BOULEZ'S BOOKS!
AND WHO IS THE LOVELY *MADEMOISELLE* WITH WHOM YOU ARE TRAVELING?
GOOD EVENING, *MONSIEUR* BOULEZ.
LIZ SHERMAN.
I SEE. YOU HAVE THE POWER OF FIRE, *OUI*?
HOW DID YOU KNOW?

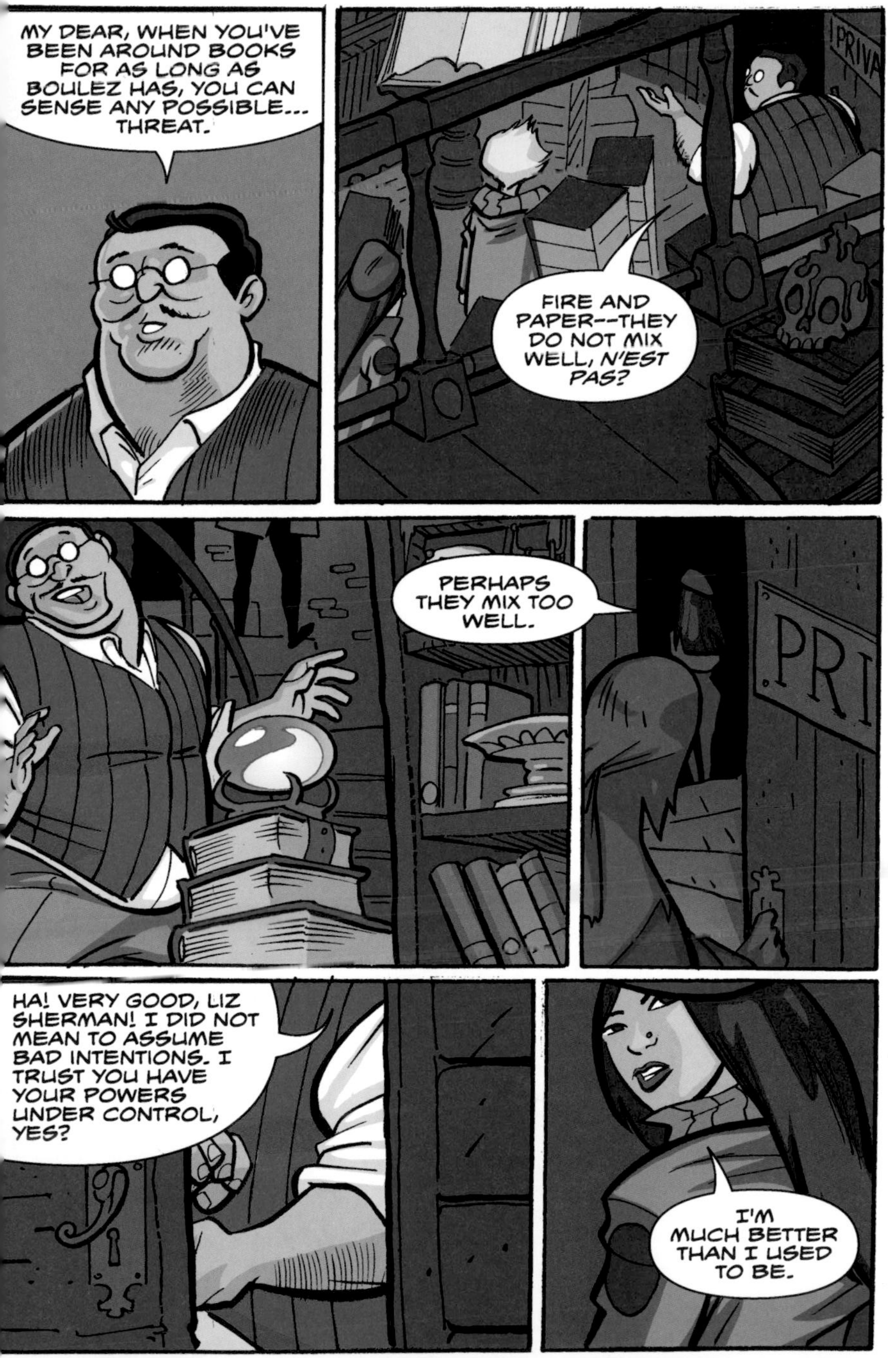
MY DEAR, WHEN YOU'VE BEEN AROUND BOOKS FOR AS LONG AS BOULEZ HAS, YOU CAN SENSE ANY POSSIBLE... THREAT.
PRIVA
FIRE AND PAPER--THEY DO NOT MIX WELL, *N'EST PAS?*
PERHAPS THEY MIX TOO WELL.
PRI
HA! VERY GOOD, LIZ SHERMAN! I DID NOT MEAN TO ASSUME BAD INTENTIONS. I TRUST YOU HAVE YOUR POWERS UNDER CONTROL, YES?
I'M MUCH BETTER THAN I USED TO BE.

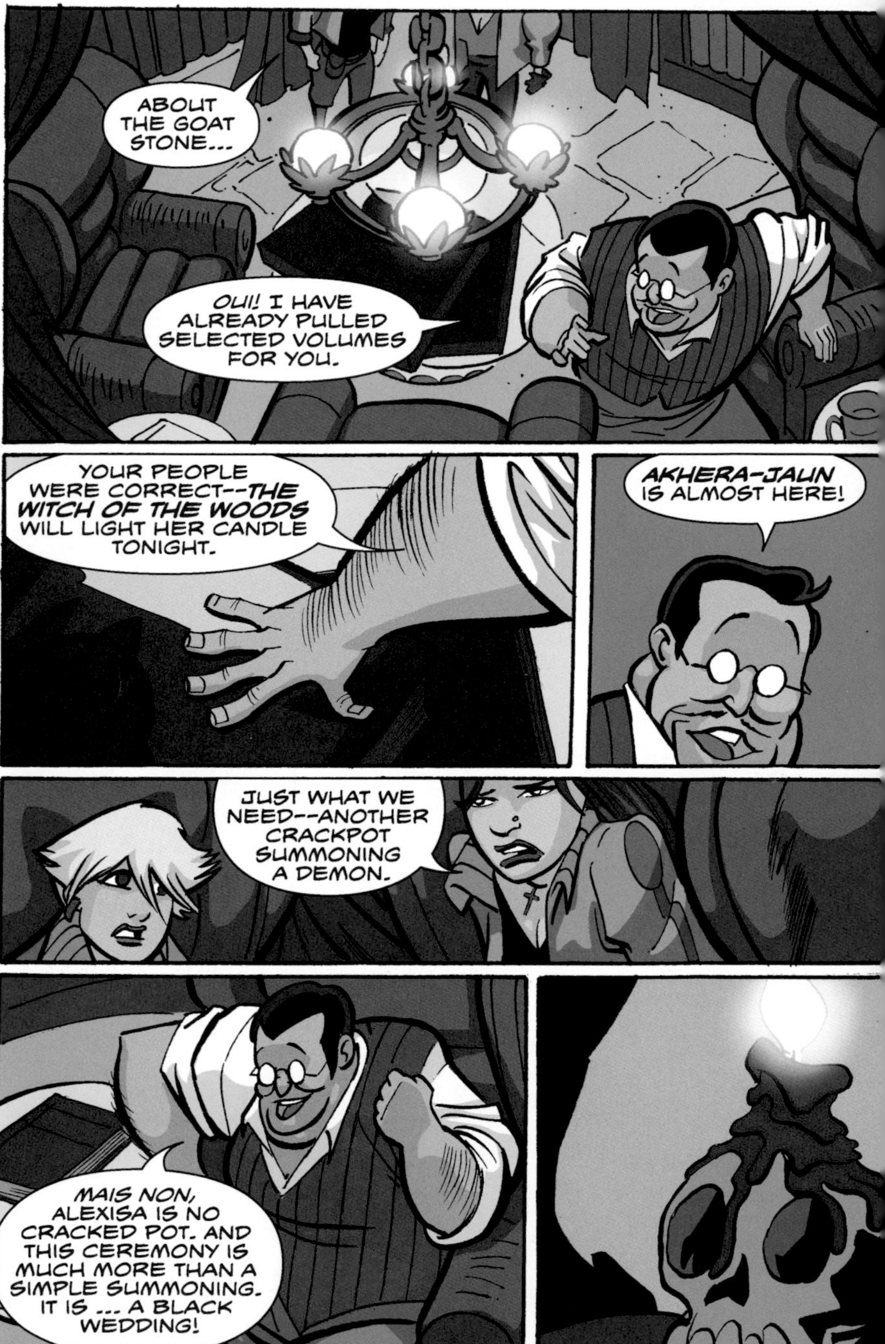
ABOUT THE GOAT STONE...
OUI! I HAVE ALREADY PULLED SELECTED VOLUMES FOR YOU.
YOUR PEOPLE WERE CORRECT--*THE WITCH OF THE WOODS* WILL LIGHT HER CANDLE TONIGHT.
AKHERA-JAUN IS ALMOST HERE!
JUST WHAT WE NEED--ANOTHER CRACKPOT SUMMONING A DEMON.
MAIS NON, ALEXISA IS NO CRACKED POT. AND THIS CEREMONY IS MUCH MORE THAN A SIMPLE SUMMONING. IT IS ... A BLACK WEDDING!

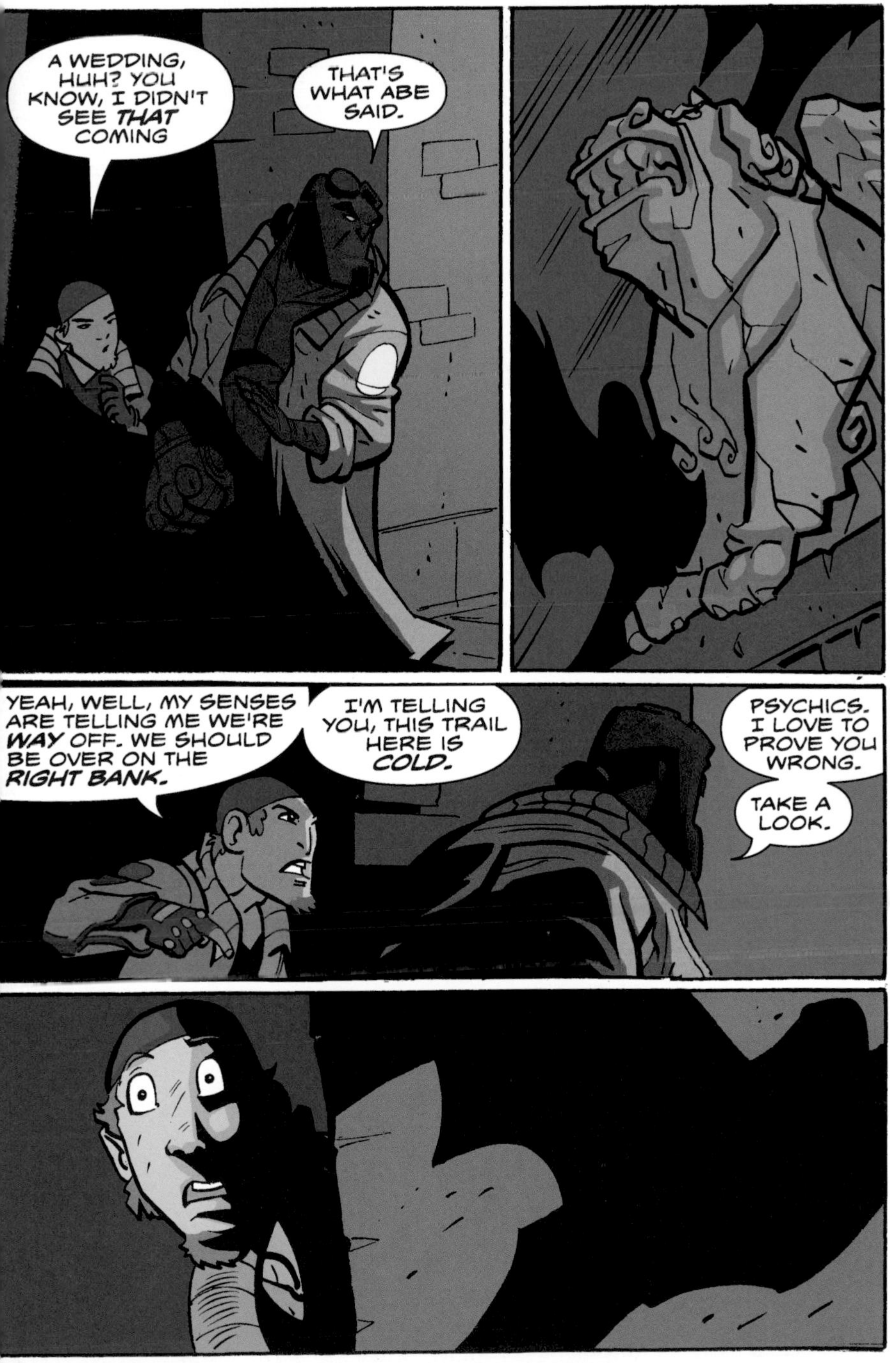
A WEDDING, HUH? YOU KNOW, I DIDN'T SEE *THAT* COMING
THAT'S WHAT ABE SAID.
YEAH, WELL, MY SENSES ARE TELLING ME WE'RE *WAY* OFF. WE SHOULD BE OVER ON THE *RIGHT BANK.*
I'M TELLING YOU, THIS TRAIL HERE IS *COLD.*
PSYCHICS. I LOVE TO PROVE YOU WRONG.
TAKE A LOOK.

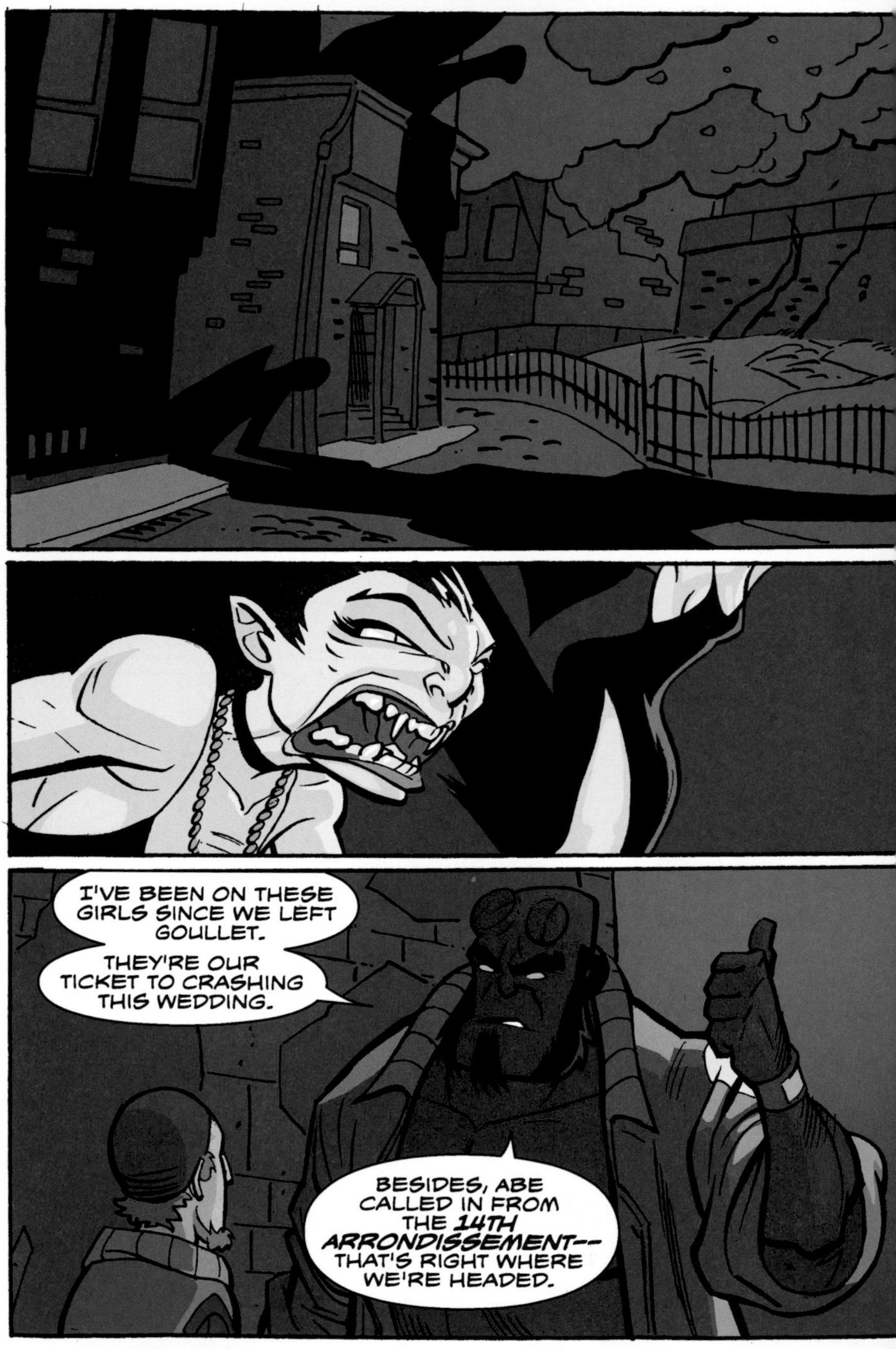
I'VE BEEN ON THESE GIRLS SINCE WE LEFT GOULLET.
THEY'RE OUR TICKET TO CRASHING THIS WEDDING.
BESIDES, ABE CALLED IN FROM THE *14TH ARRONDISSEMENT*-- THAT'S RIGHT WHERE WE'RE HEADED.

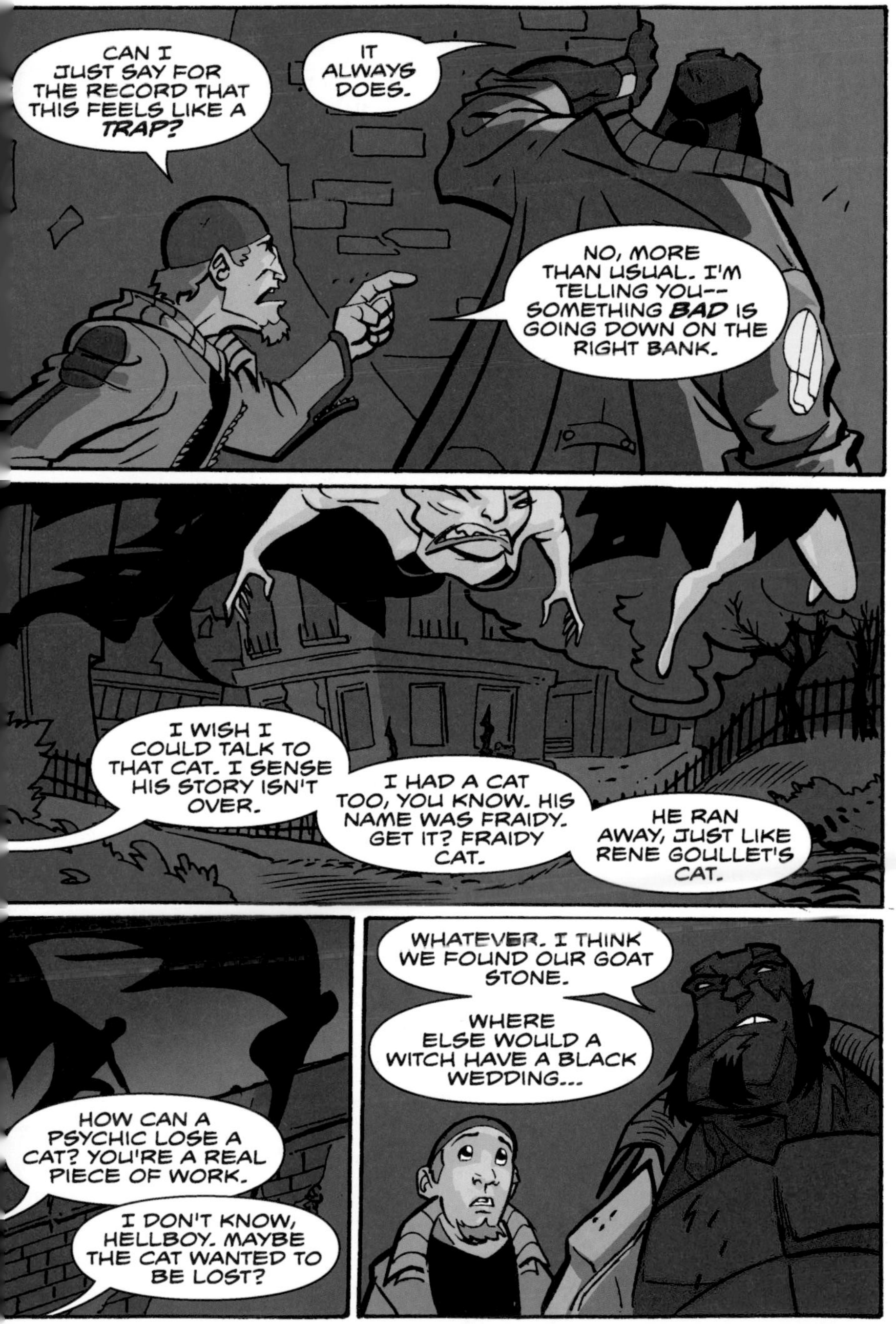
CAN I JUST SAY FOR THE RECORD THAT THIS FEELS LIKE A *TRAP?*
IT ALWAYS DOES.
NO, MORE THAN USUAL. I'M TELLING YOU-- SOMETHING ***BAD*** IS GOING DOWN ON THE RIGHT BANK.
I WISH I COULD TALK TO THAT CAT. I SENSE HIS STORY ISN'T OVER.
I HAD A CAT TOO, YOU KNOW. HIS NAME WAS FRAIDY. GET IT? FRAIDY CAT.
HE RAN AWAY, JUST LIKE RENE GOULLET'S CAT.
HOW CAN A PSYCHIC LOSE A CAT? YOU'RE A REAL PIECE OF WORK.
I DON'T KNOW, HELLBOY. MAYBE THE CAT WANTED TO BE LOST?
WHATEVER. I THINK WE FOUND OUR GOAT STONE.
WHERE ELSE WOULD A WITCH HAVE A BLACK WEDDING...

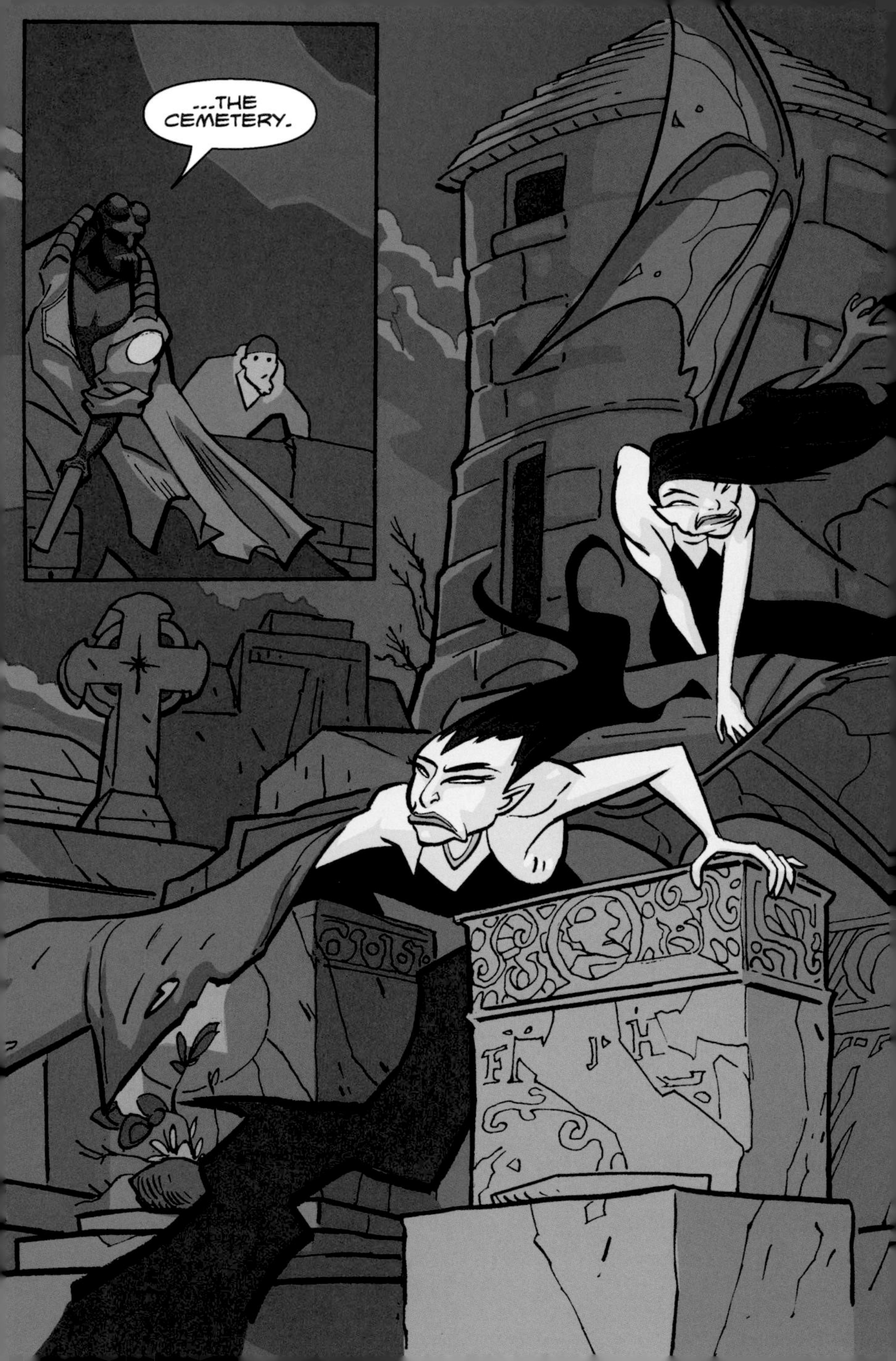
...THE CEMETERY.

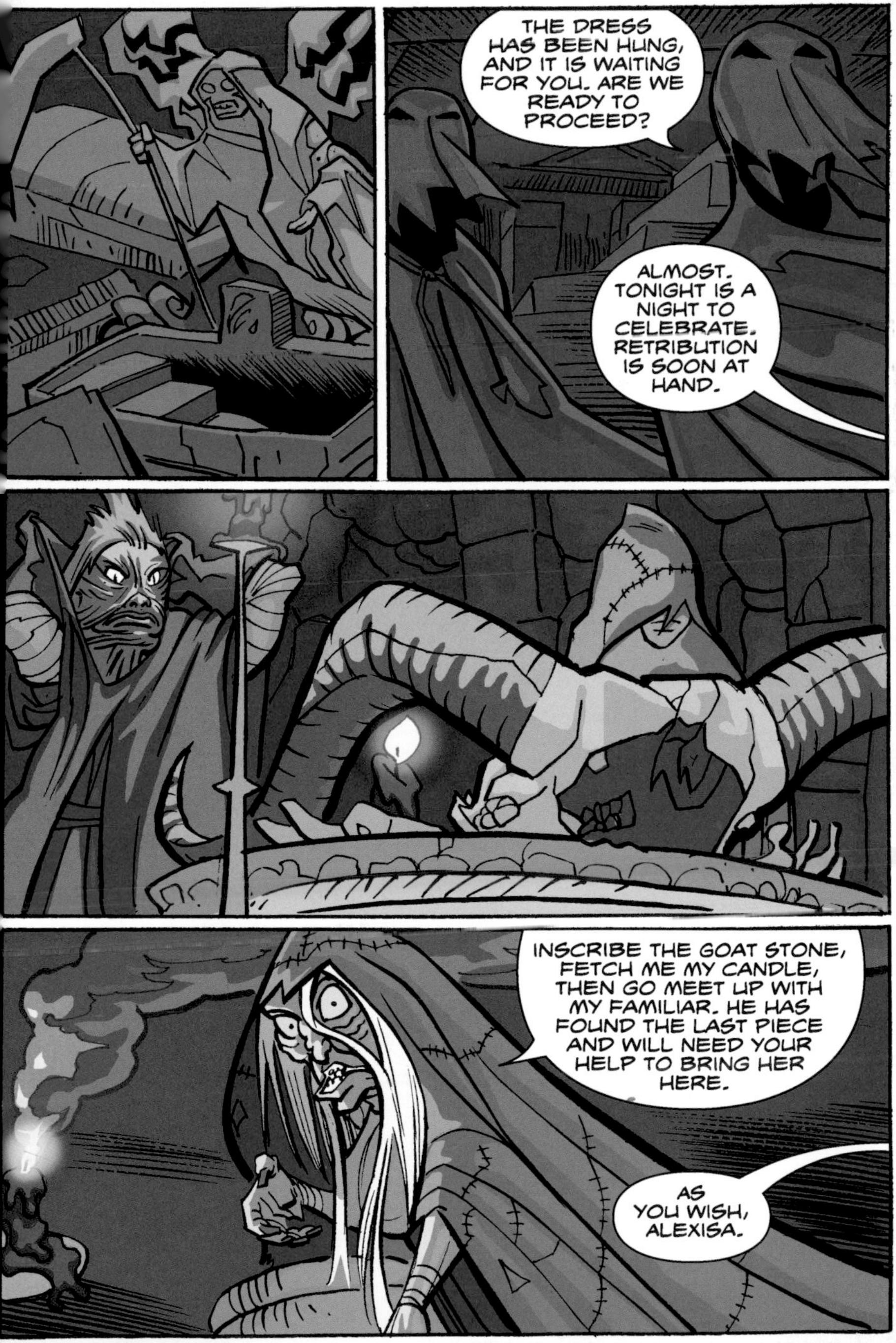
THE DRESS HAS BEEN HUNG, AND IT IS WAITING FOR YOU. ARE WE READY TO PROCEED?
ALMOST. TONIGHT IS A NIGHT TO CELEBRATE. RETRIBUTION IS SOON AT HAND.
INSCRIBE THE GOAT STONE, FETCH ME MY CANDLE, THEN GO MEET UP WITH MY FAMILIAR. HE HAS FOUND THE LAST PIECE AND WILL NEED YOUR HELP TO BRING HER HERE.
AS YOU WISH, ALEXISA.

FOOOSH

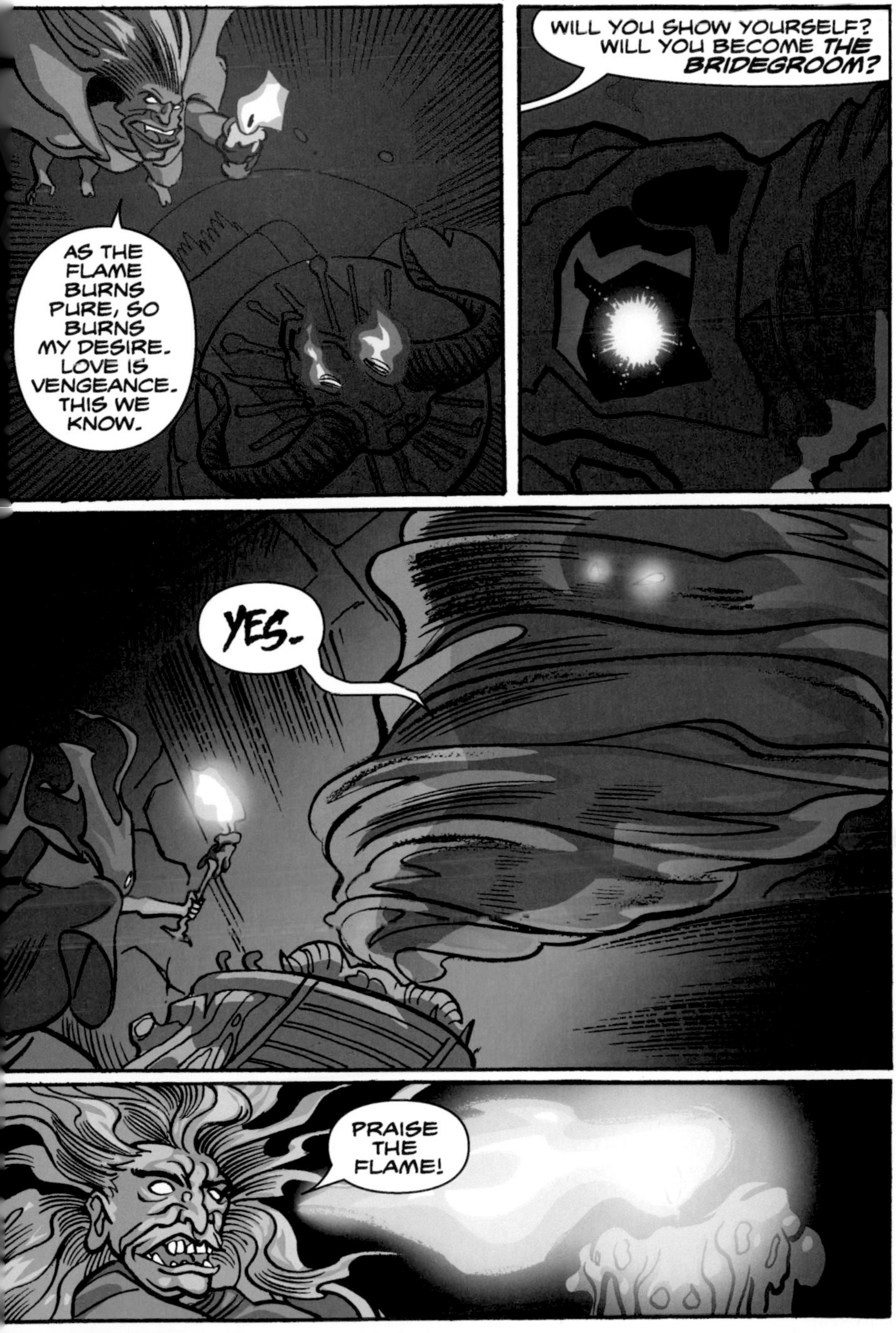
AS THE FLAME BURNS PURE, SO BURNS MY DESIRE. LOVE IS VENGEANCE. THIS WE KNOW.
WILL YOU SHOW YOURSELF? WILL YOU BECOME THE BRIDEGROOM?
YES.
PRAISE THE FLAME!

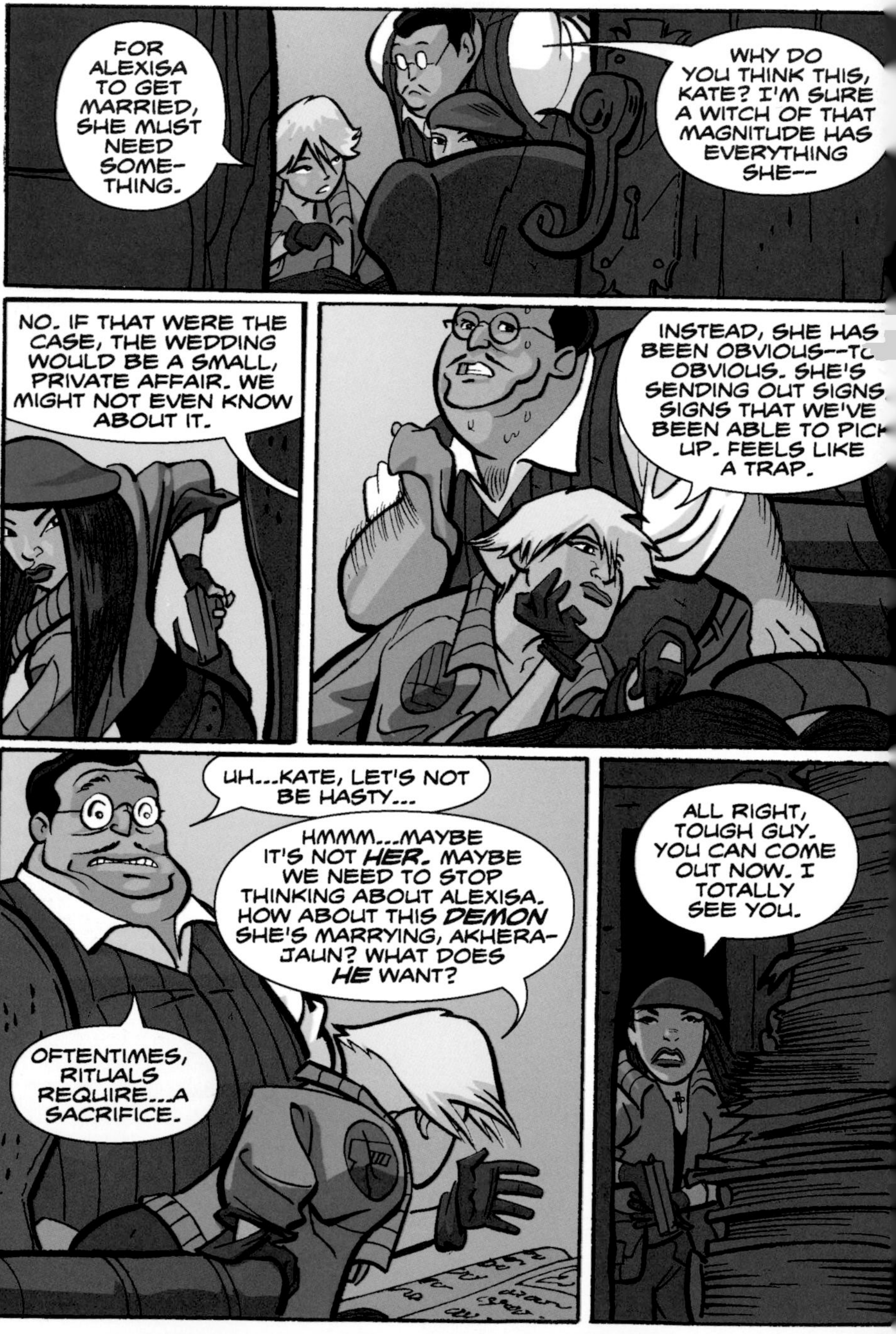
FOR ALEXISA TO GET MARRIED, SHE MUST NEED SOME-THING.
WHY DO YOU THINK THIS, KATE? I'M SURE A WITCH OF THAT MAGNITUDE HAS EVERYTHING SHE--
NO. IF THAT WERE THE CASE, THE WEDDING WOULD BE A SMALL, PRIVATE AFFAIR. WE MIGHT NOT EVEN KNOW ABOUT IT.
INSTEAD, SHE HAS BEEN OBVIOUS--TO OBVIOUS. SHE'S SENDING OUT SIGNS SIGNS THAT WE'VE BEEN ABLE TO PICK UP. FEELS LIKE A TRAP.
UH...KATE, LET'S NOT BE HASTY...
HMMM...MAYBE IT'S NOT *HER*. MAYBE WE NEED TO STOP THINKING ABOUT ALEXISA. HOW ABOUT THIS *DEMON* SHE'S MARRYING, AKHERA-JAUN? WHAT DOES *HE* WANT?
OFTENTIMES, RITUALS REQUIRE...A SACRIFICE.
ALL RIGHT, TOUGH GUY. YOU CAN COME OUT NOW. I TOTALLY SEE YOU.

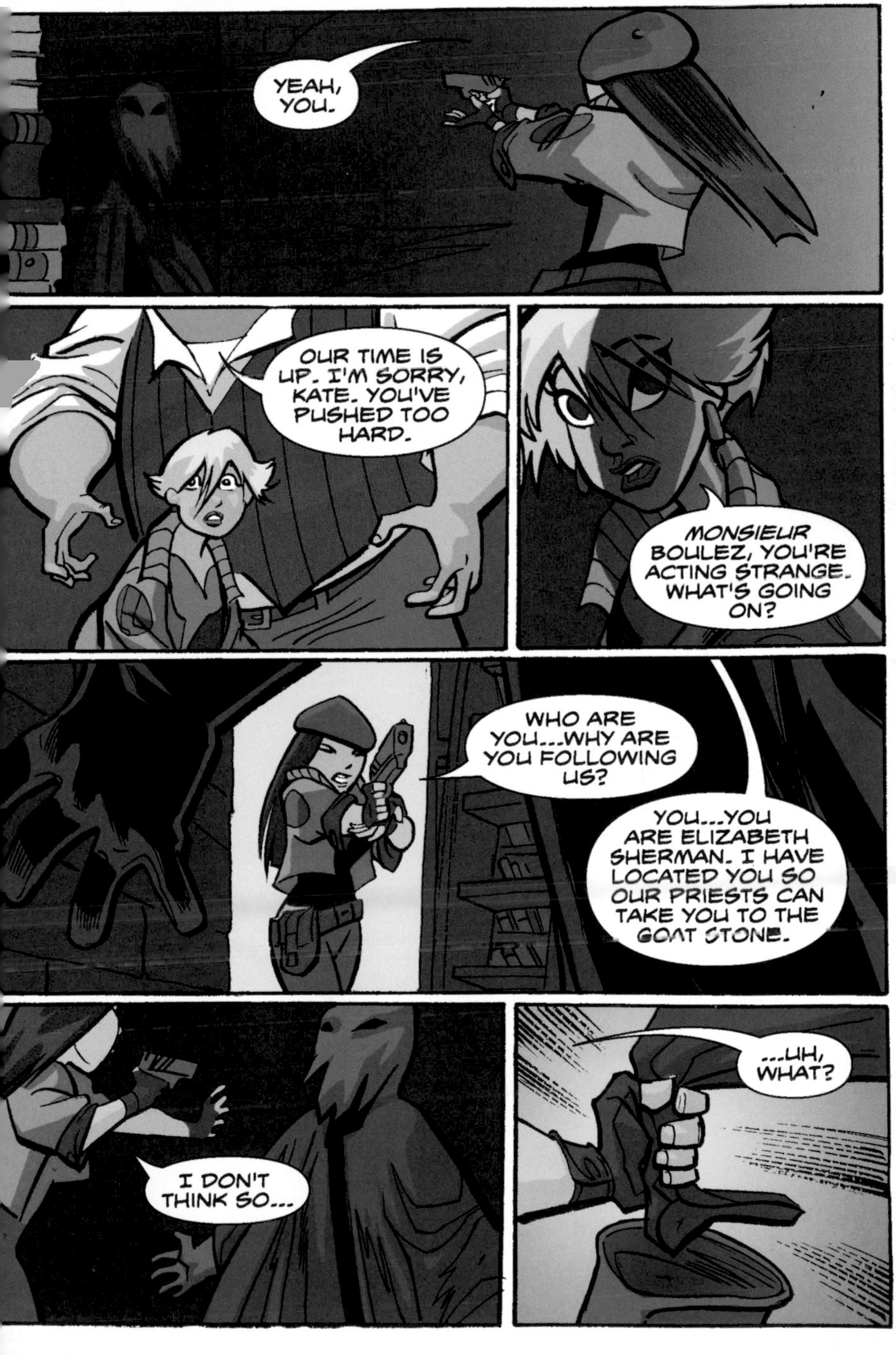
YEAH, YOU.
OUR TIME IS UP. I'M SORRY, KATE. YOU'VE PUSHED TOO HARD.
MONSIEUR BOULEZ, YOU'RE ACTING STRANGE. WHAT'S GOING ON?
WHO ARE YOU...WHY ARE YOU FOLLOWING US?
YOU...YOU ARE ELIZABETH SHERMAN. I HAVE LOCATED YOU SO OUR PRIESTS CAN TAKE YOU TO THE GOAT STONE.
I DON'T THINK SO...
...UH, WHAT?

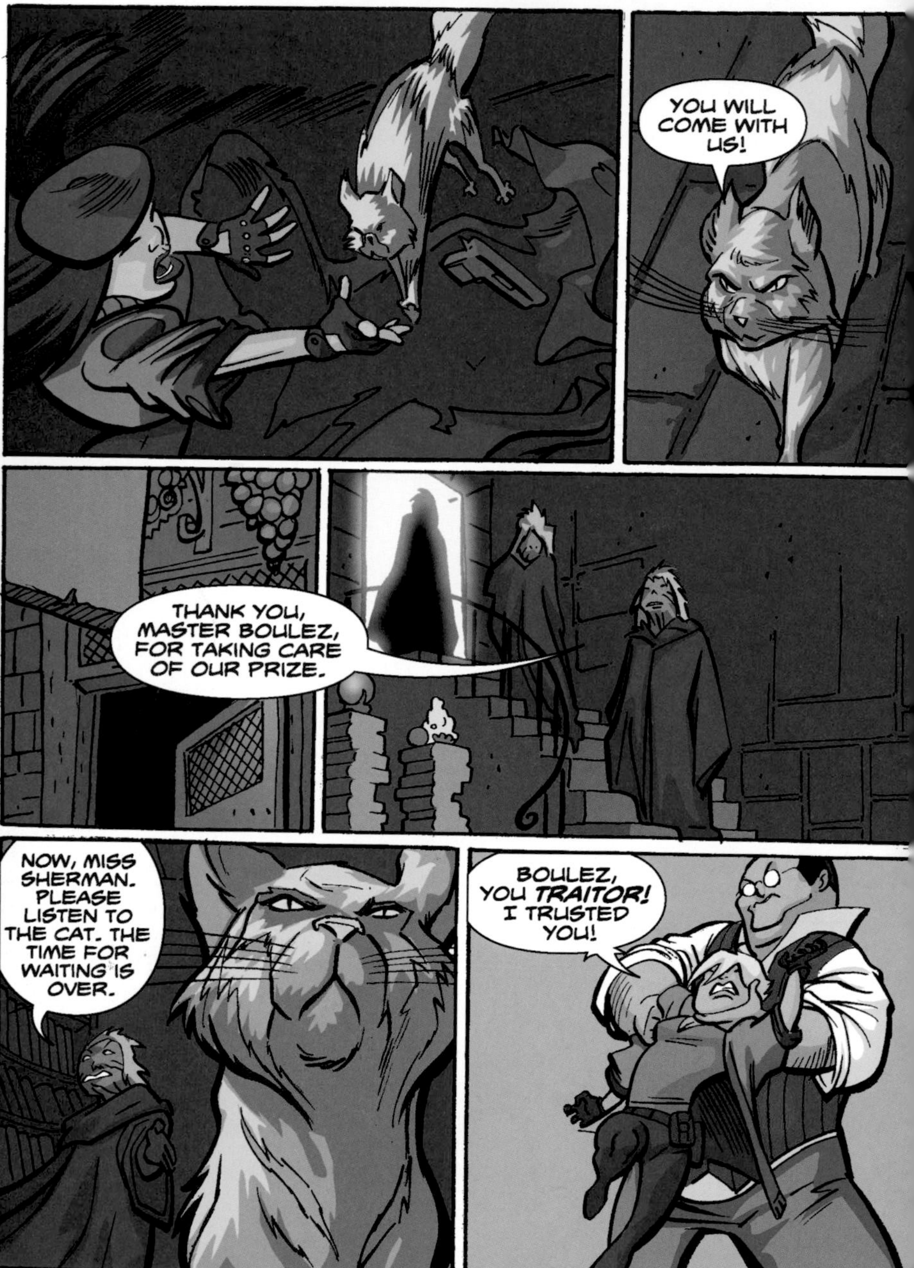
YOU WILL COME WITH US!
THANK YOU, MASTER BOULEZ, FOR TAKING CARE OF OUR PRIZE.
NOW, MISS SHERMAN. PLEASE LISTEN TO THE CAT. THE TIME FOR WAITING IS OVER.
BOULEZ, YOU *TRAITOR*! I TRUSTED YOU!

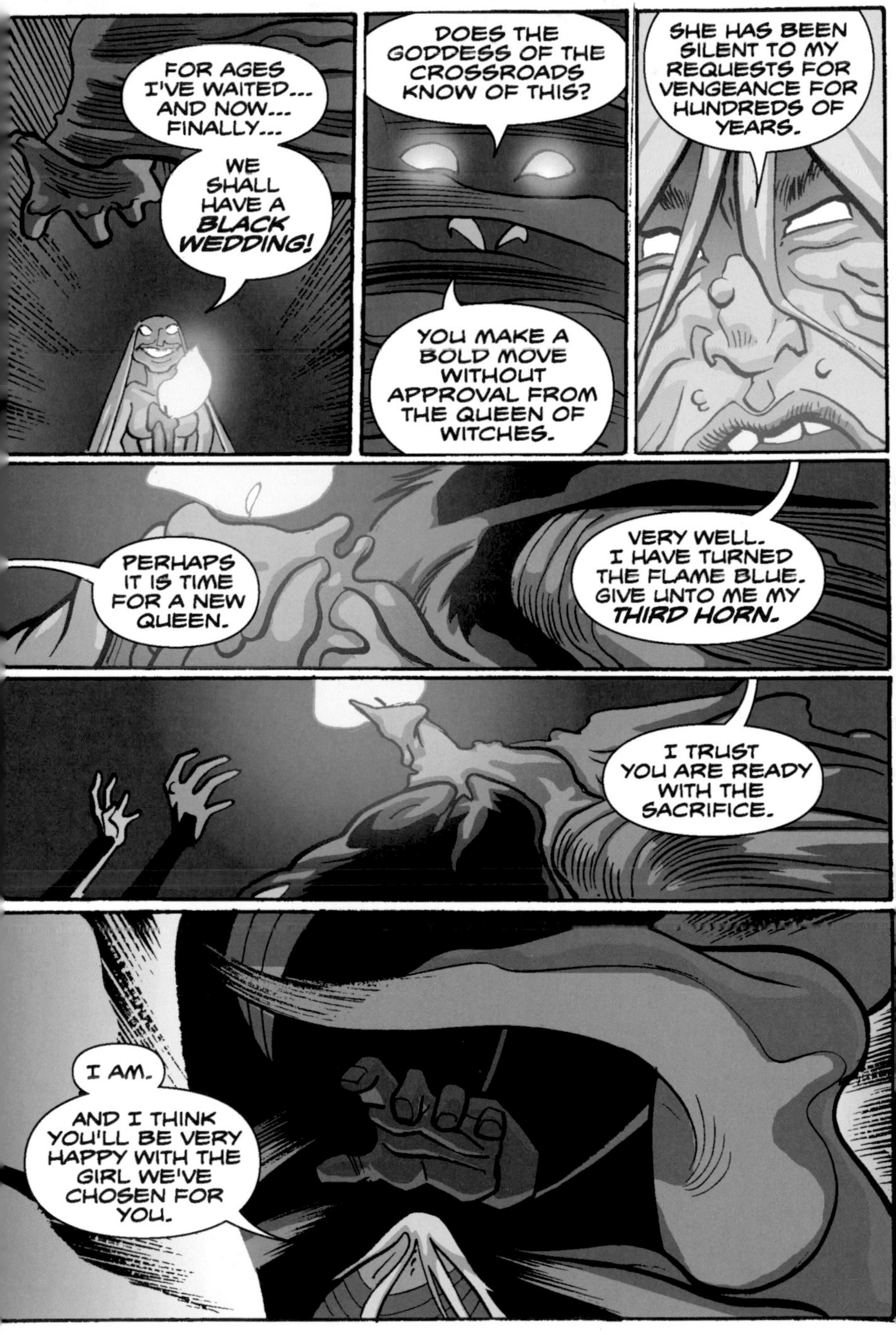

FOR AGES I'VE WAITED... AND NOW... FINALLY...
WE SHALL HAVE A *BLACK WEDDING!*
DOES THE GODDESS OF THE CROSSROADS KNOW OF THIS?
YOU MAKE A BOLD MOVE WITHOUT APPROVAL FROM THE QUEEN OF WITCHES.
SHE HAS BEEN SILENT TO MY REQUESTS FOR VENGEANCE FOR HUNDREDS OF YEARS.
PERHAPS IT IS TIME FOR A NEW QUEEN.
VERY WELL. I HAVE TURNED THE FLAME BLUE. GIVE UNTO ME MY *THIRD HORN.*
I TRUST YOU ARE READY WITH THE SACRIFICE.
I AM.
AND I THINK YOU'LL BE VERY HAPPY WITH THE GIRL WE'VE CHOSEN FOR YOU.

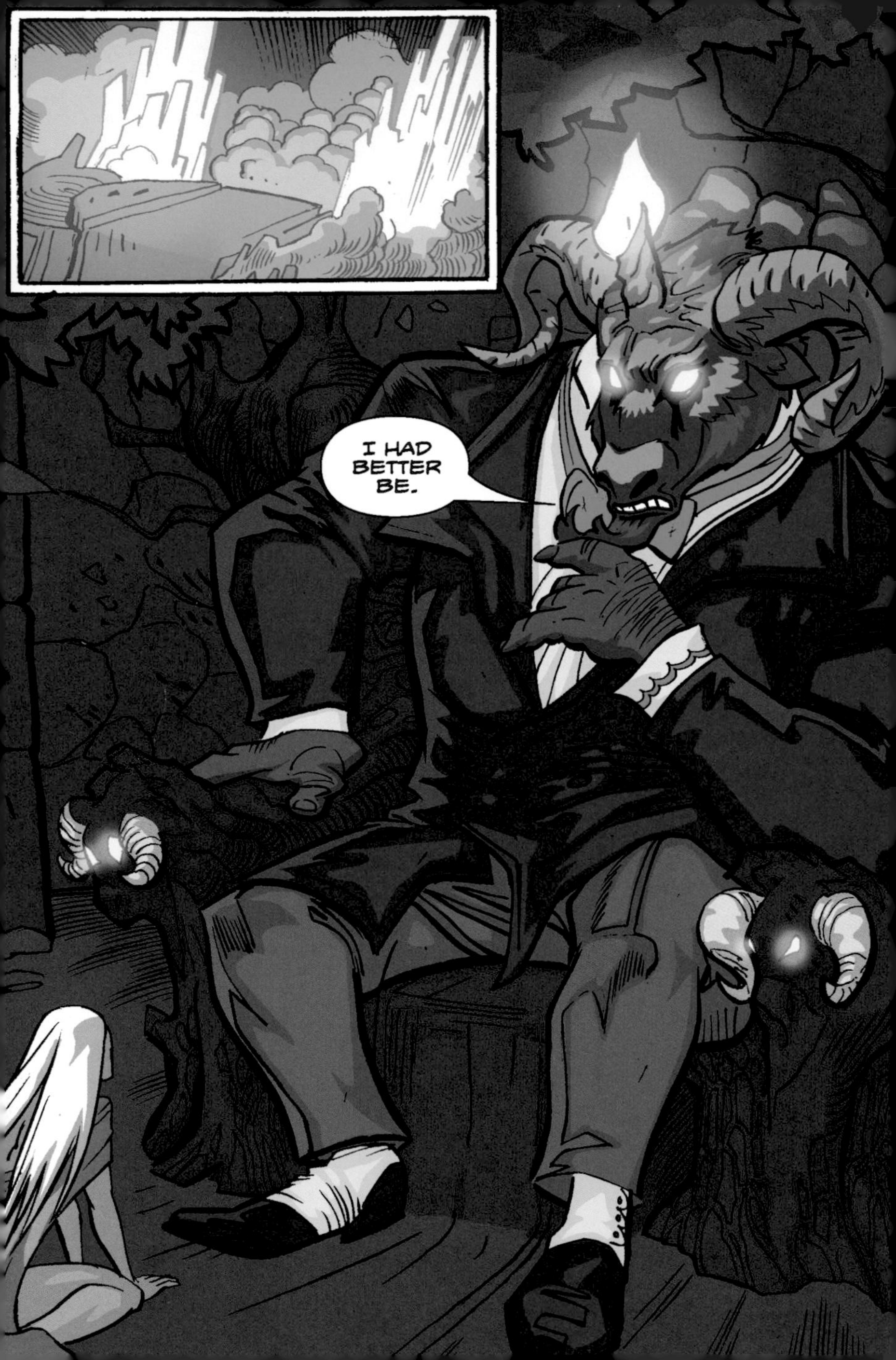
I HAD BETTER BE.

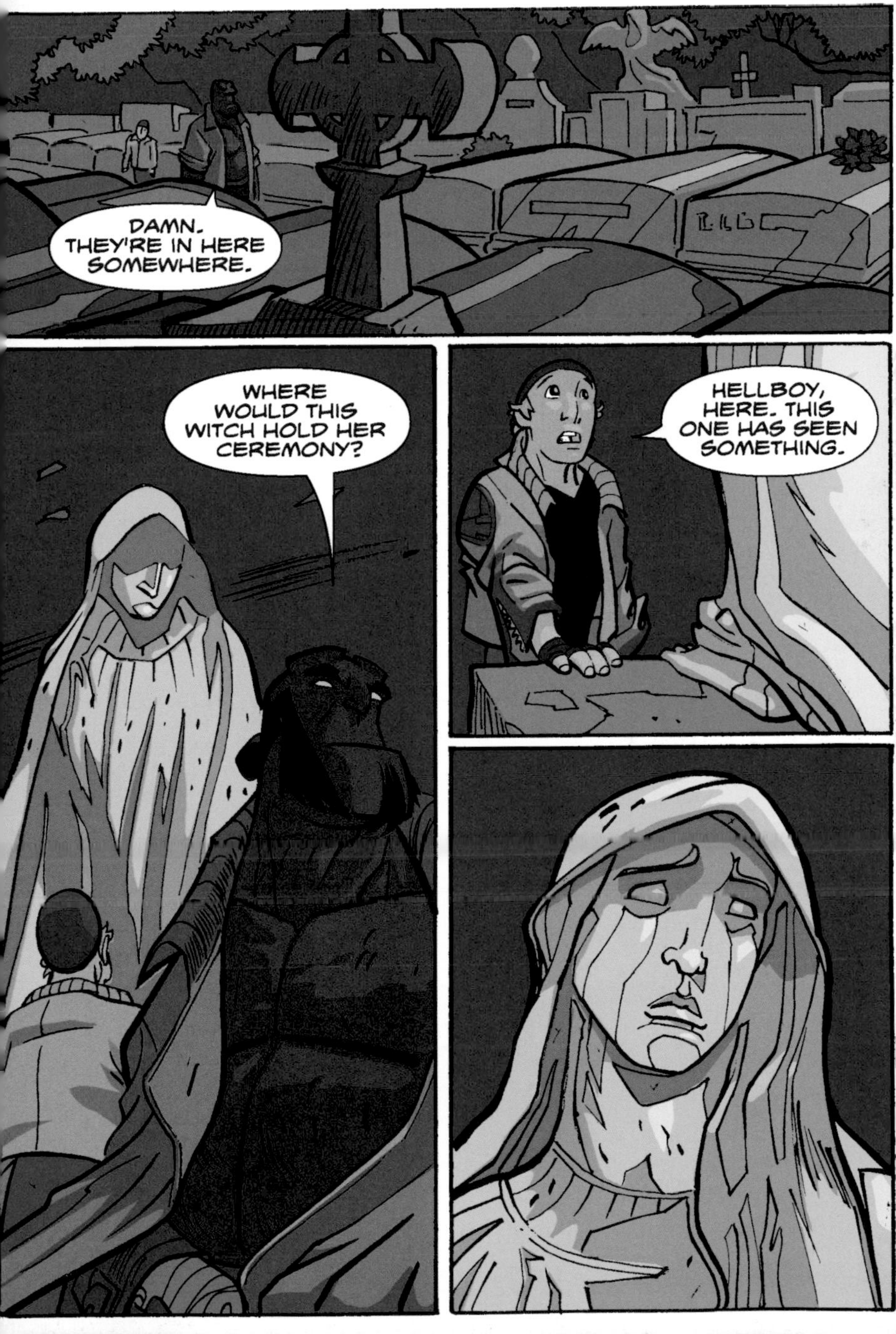
DAMN. THEY'RE IN HERE SOMEWHERE.
WHERE WOULD THIS WITCH HOLD HER CEREMONY?
HELLBOY, HERE. THIS ONE HAS SEEN SOMETHING.

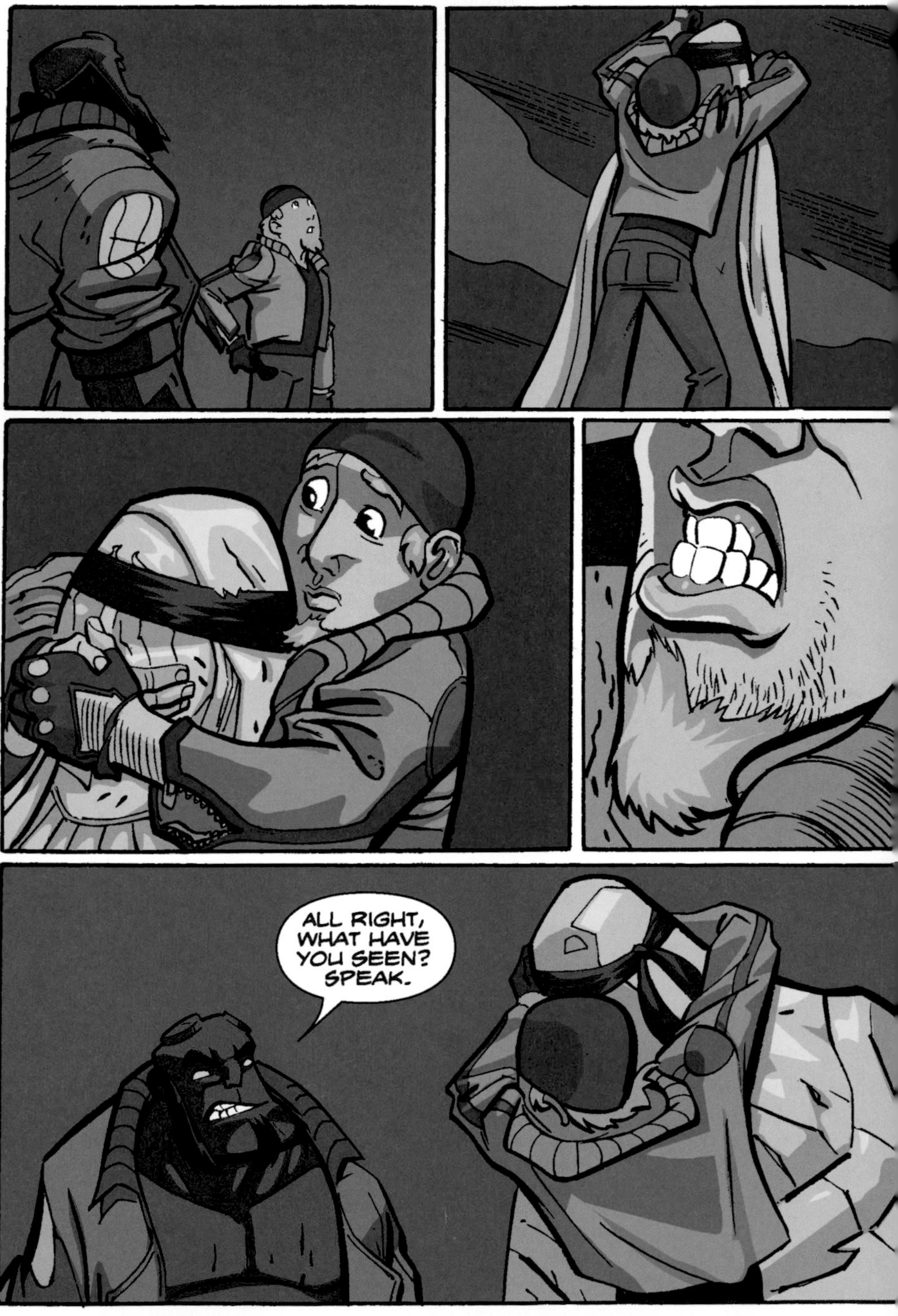
ALL RIGHT, WHAT HAVE YOU SEEN? SPEAK.

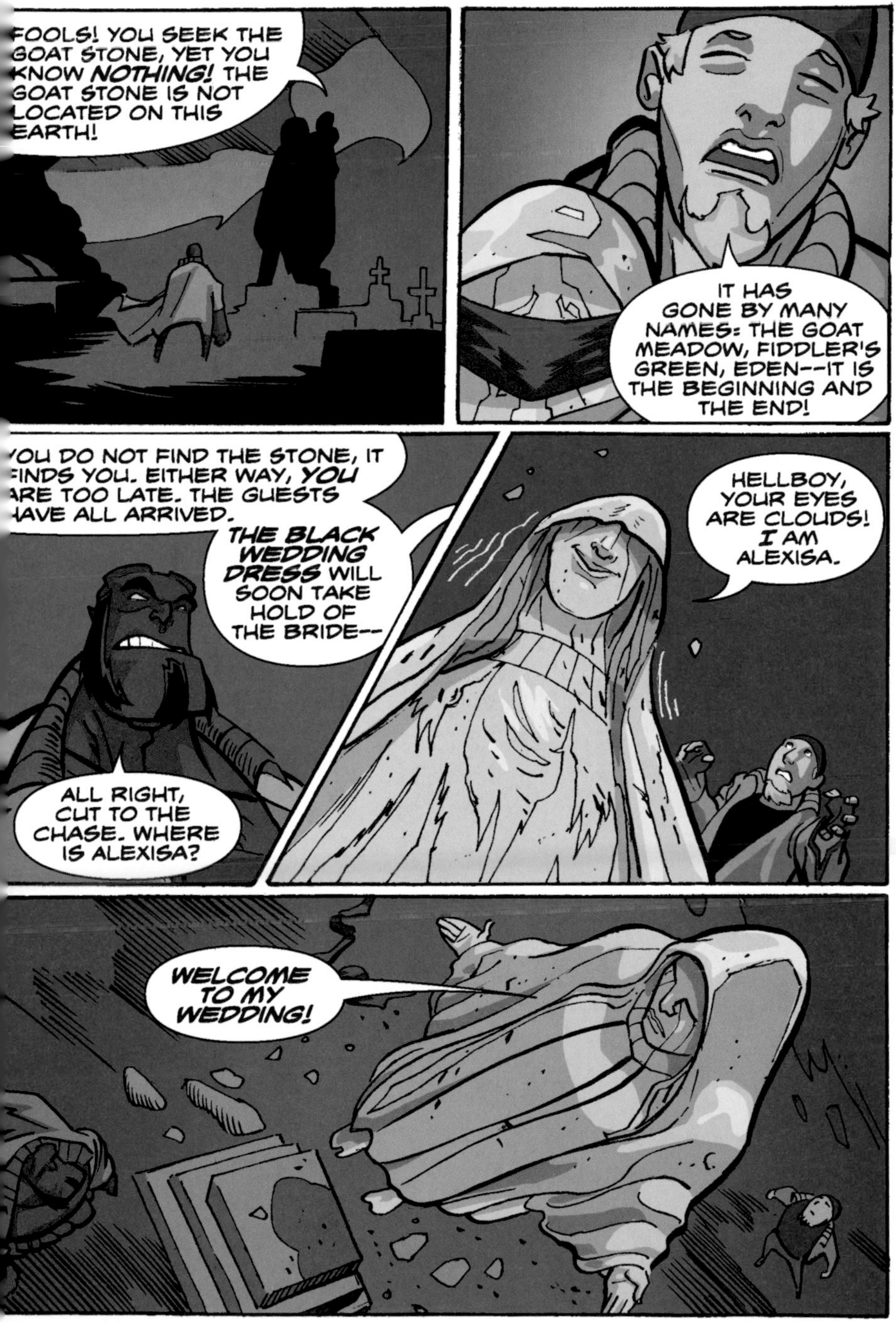
FOOLS! YOU SEEK THE GOAT STONE, YET YOU KNOW NOTHING! THE GOAT STONE IS NOT LOCATED ON THIS EARTH!
IT HAS GONE BY MANY NAMES: THE GOAT MEADOW, FIDDLER'S GREEN, EDEN--IT IS THE BEGINNING AND THE END!
YOU DO NOT FIND THE STONE, IT FINDS YOU. EITHER WAY, YOU ARE TOO LATE. THE GUESTS HAVE ALL ARRIVED.
THE BLACK WEDDING DRESS WILL SOON TAKE HOLD OF THE BRIDE--
ALL RIGHT, CUT TO THE CHASE. WHERE IS ALEXISA?
HELLBOY, YOUR EYES ARE CLOUDS! I AM ALEXISA.
WELCOME TO MY WEDDING!

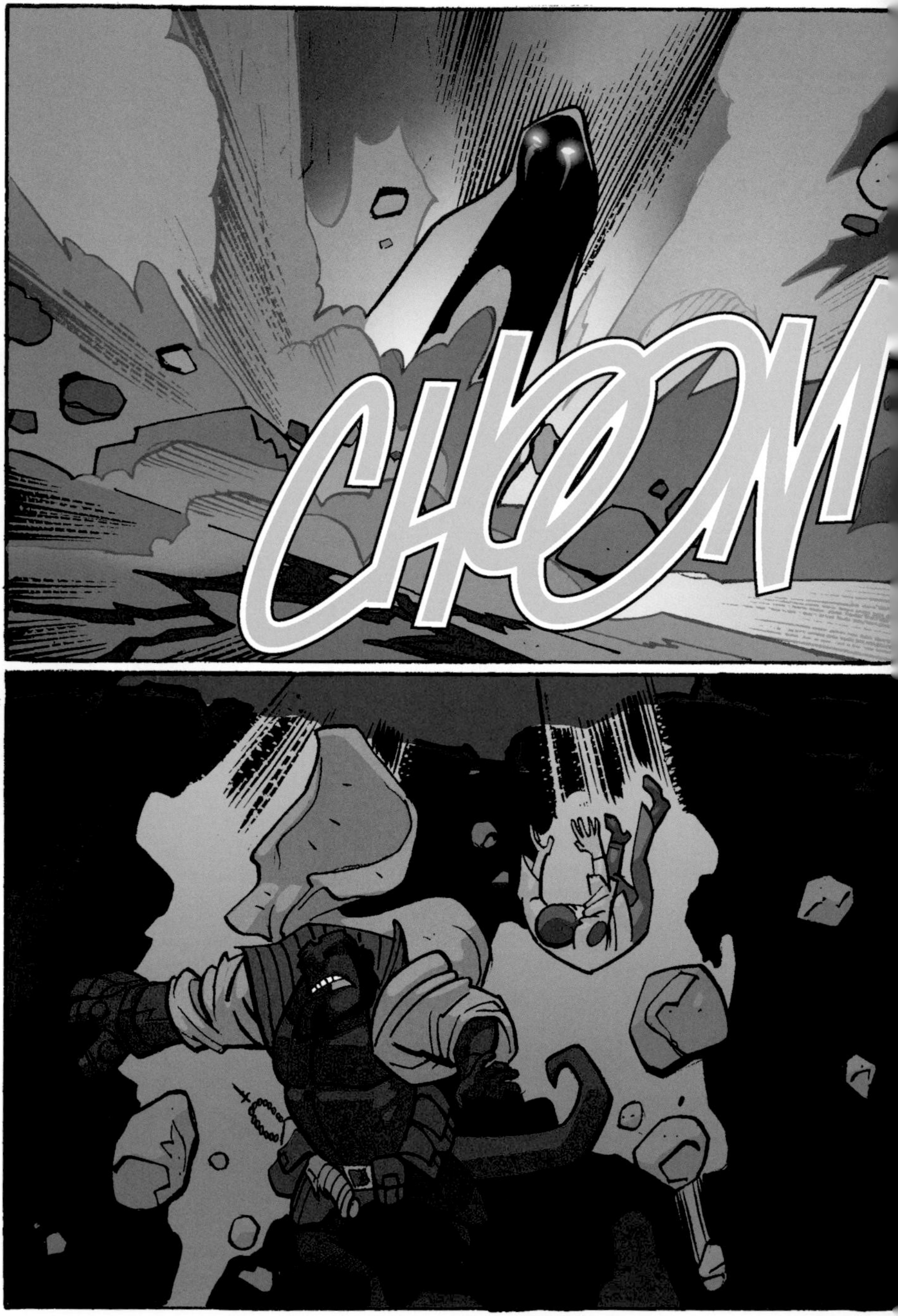
CHOOM

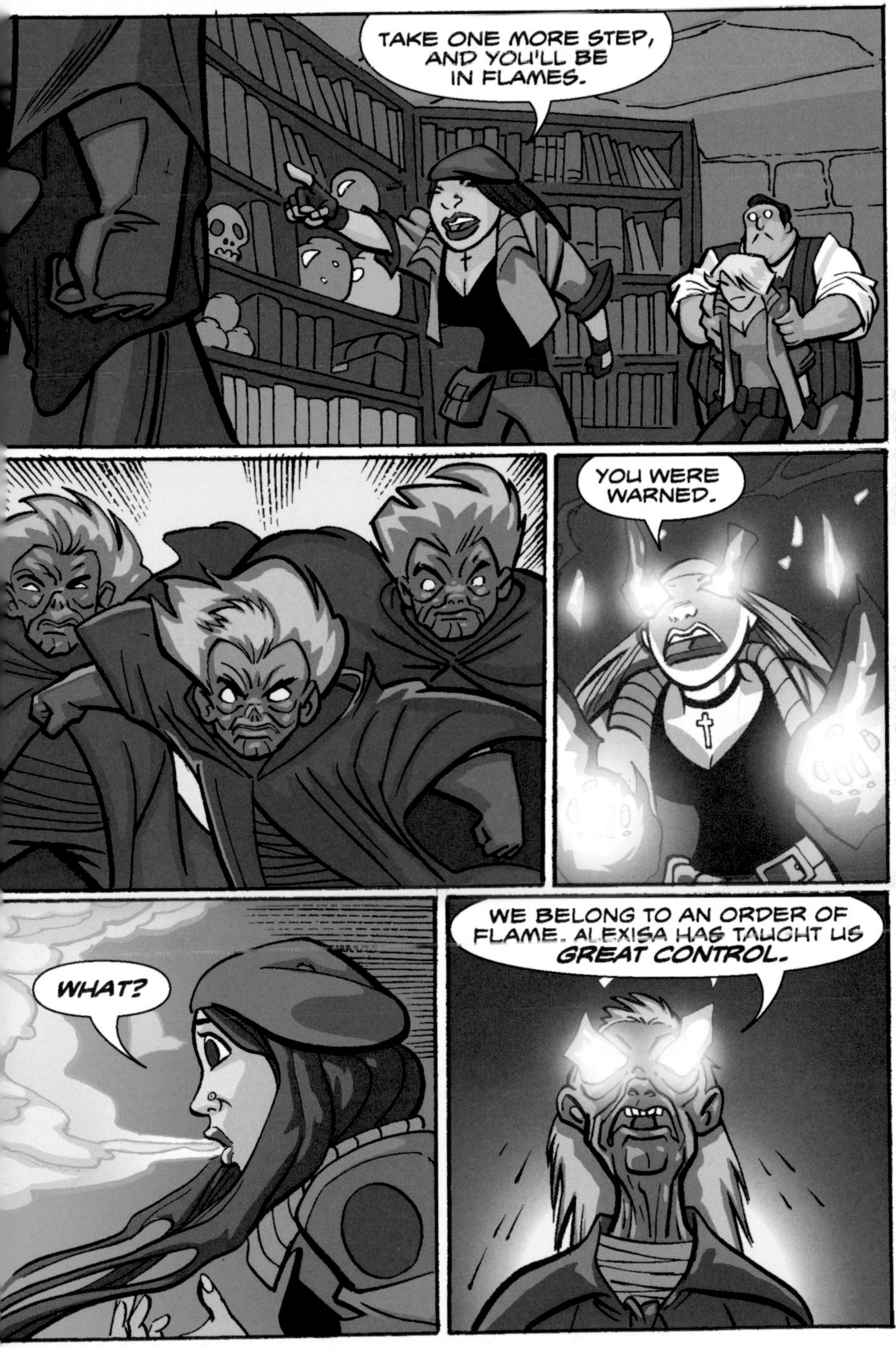
TAKE ONE MORE STEP, AND YOU'LL BE IN FLAMES.
YOU WERE WARNED.
WHAT?
WE BELONG TO AN ORDER OF FLAME. ALEXISA HAS TAUGHT US *GREAT CONTROL*.

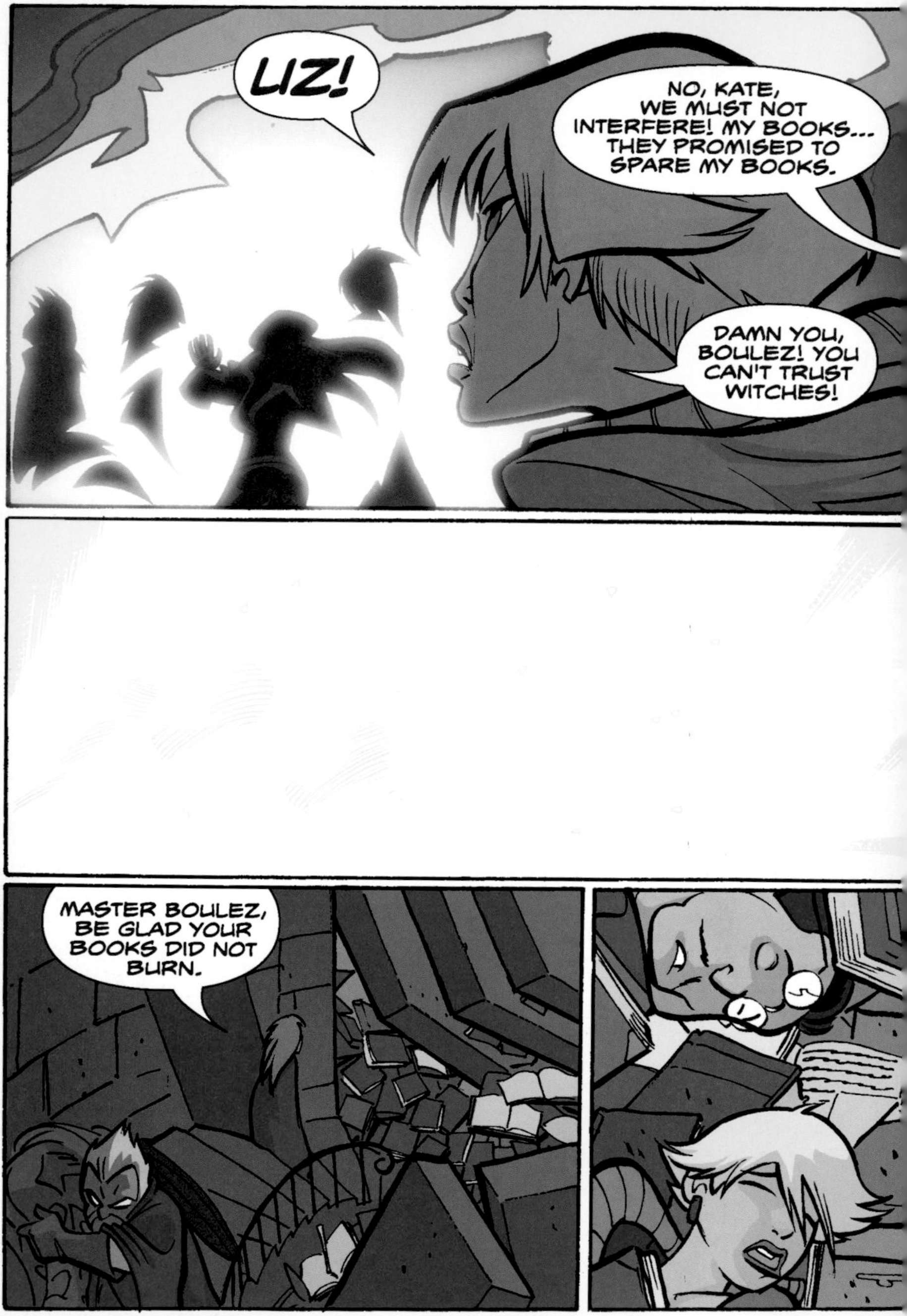
LIZ!
NO, KATE, WE MUST NOT INTERFERE! MY BOOKS... THEY PROMISED TO SPARE MY BOOKS.
DAMN YOU, BOULEZ! YOU CAN'T TRUST WITCHES!
MASTER BOULEZ, BE GLAD YOUR BOOKS DID NOT BURN.

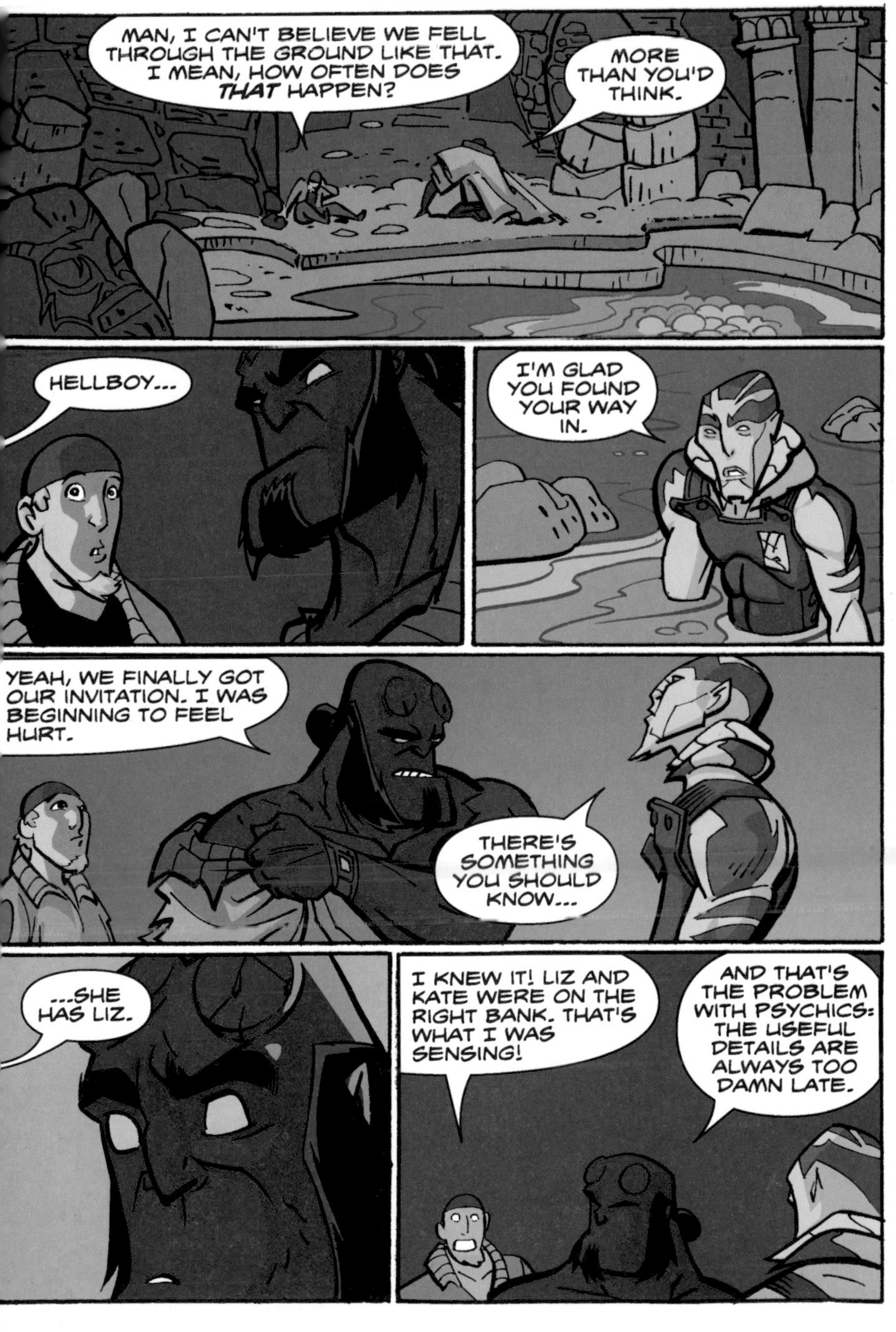
MAN, I CAN'T BELIEVE WE FELL THROUGH THE GROUND LIKE THAT. I MEAN, HOW OFTEN DOES *THAT* HAPPEN?
MORE THAN YOU'D THINK.
HELLBOY...
I'M GLAD YOU FOUND YOUR WAY IN.
YEAH, WE FINALLY GOT OUR INVITATION. I WAS BEGINNING TO FEEL HURT.
THERE'S SOMETHING YOU SHOULD KNOW...
...SHE HAS LIZ.
I KNEW IT! LIZ AND KATE WERE ON THE RIGHT BANK. THAT'S WHAT I WAS SENSING!
AND THAT'S THE PROBLEM WITH PSYCHICS: THE USEFUL DETAILS ARE ALWAYS TOO DAMN LATE.

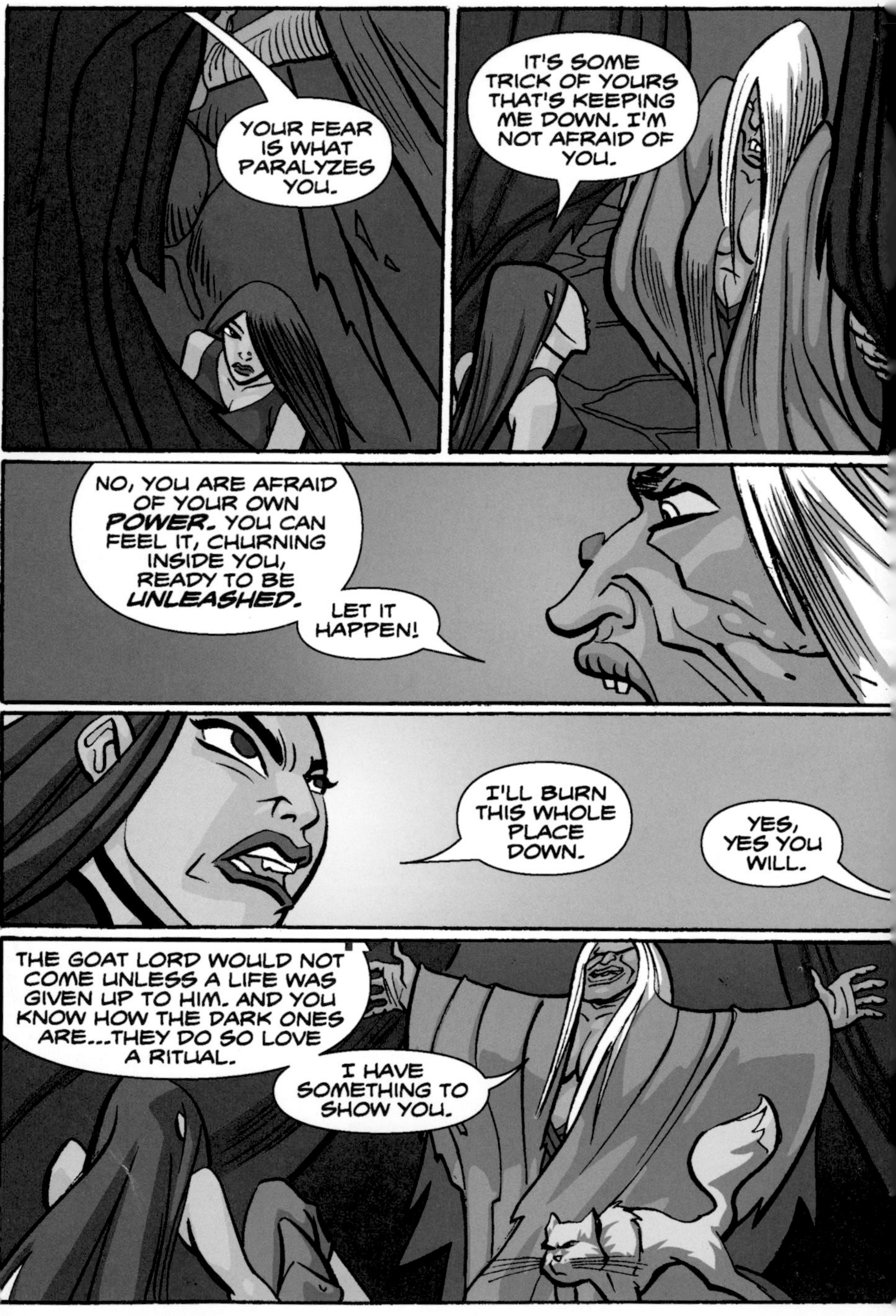
YOUR FEAR IS WHAT PARALYZES YOU.
IT'S SOME TRICK OF YOURS THAT'S KEEPING ME DOWN. I'M NOT AFRAID OF YOU.
NO, YOU ARE AFRAID OF YOUR OWN POWER. YOU CAN FEEL IT, CHURNING INSIDE YOU, READY TO BE UNLEASHED.
LET IT HAPPEN!
I'LL BURN THIS WHOLE PLACE DOWN.
YES, YES YOU WILL.
THE GOAT LORD WOULD NOT COME UNLESS A LIFE WAS GIVEN UP TO HIM. AND YOU KNOW HOW THE DARK ONES ARE...THEY DO SO LOVE A RITUAL.
I HAVE SOMETHING TO SHOW YOU.

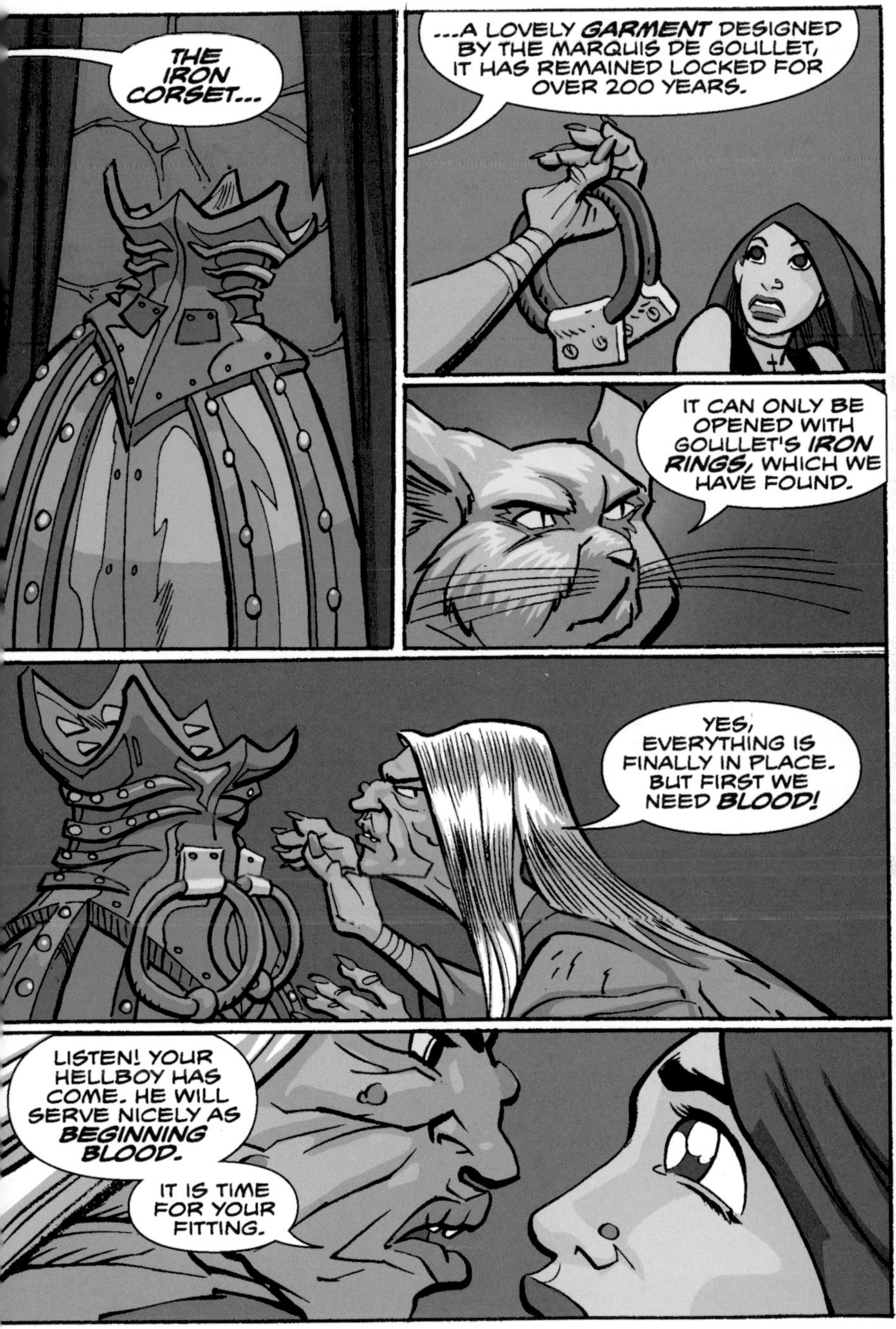
THE IRON CORSET...
...A LOVELY GARMENT DESIGNED BY THE MARQUIS DE GOULLET, IT HAS REMAINED LOCKED FOR OVER 200 YEARS.
IT CAN ONLY BE OPENED WITH GOULLET'S IRON RINGS, WHICH WE HAVE FOUND.
YES, EVERYTHING IS FINALLY IN PLACE. BUT FIRST WE NEED BLOOD!
LISTEN! YOUR HELLBOY HAS COME. HE WILL SERVE NICELY AS BEGINNING BLOOD.
IT IS TIME FOR YOUR FITTING.

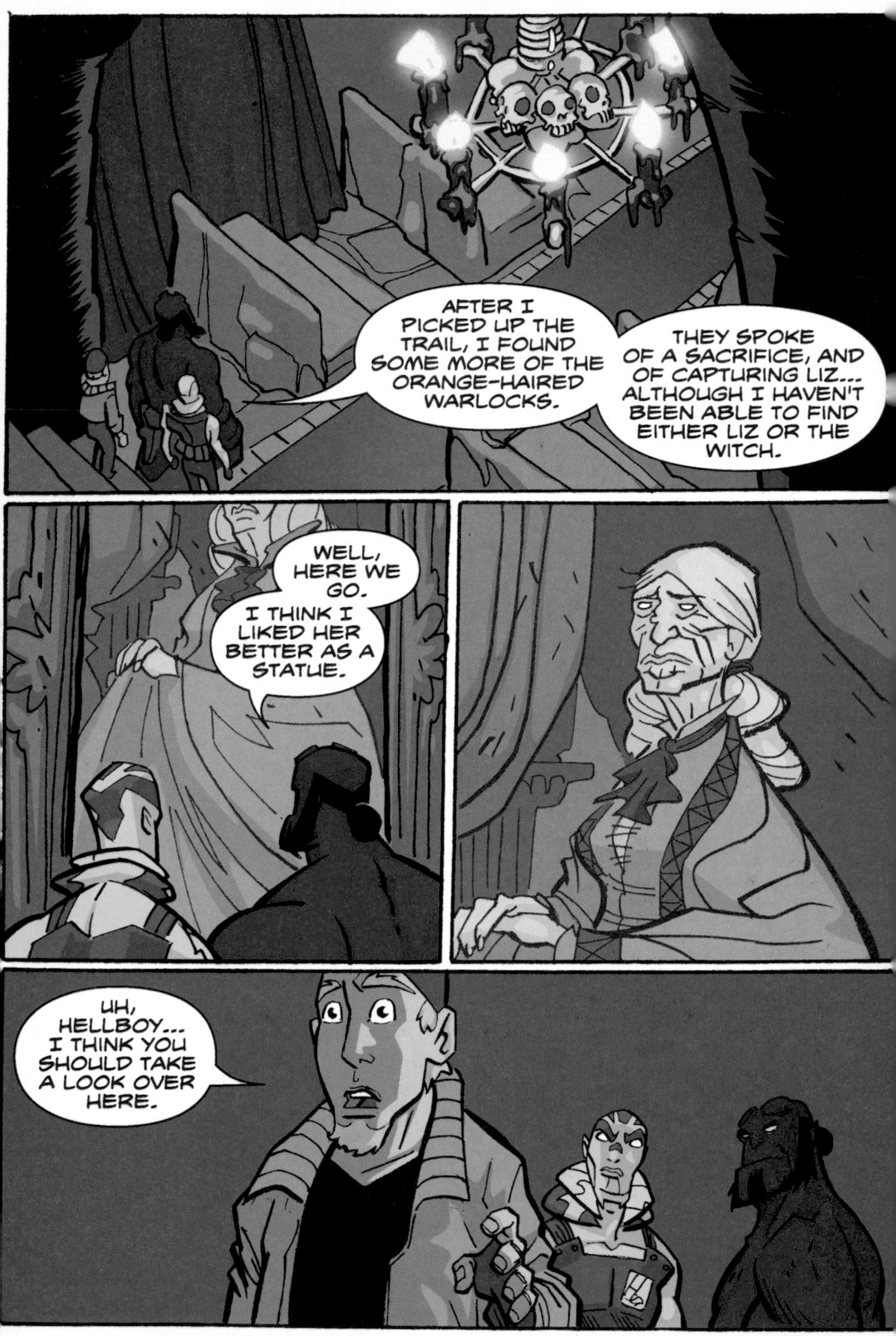
AFTER I PICKED UP THE TRAIL, I FOUND SOME MORE OF THE ORANGE-HAIRED WARLOCKS.
THEY SPOKE OF A SACRIFICE, AND OF CAPTURING LIZ... ALTHOUGH I HAVEN'T BEEN ABLE TO FIND EITHER LIZ OR THE WITCH.
WELL, HERE WE GO.
I THINK I LIKED HER BETTER AS A STATUE.
UH, HELLBOY... I THINK YOU SHOULD TAKE A LOOK OVER HERE.

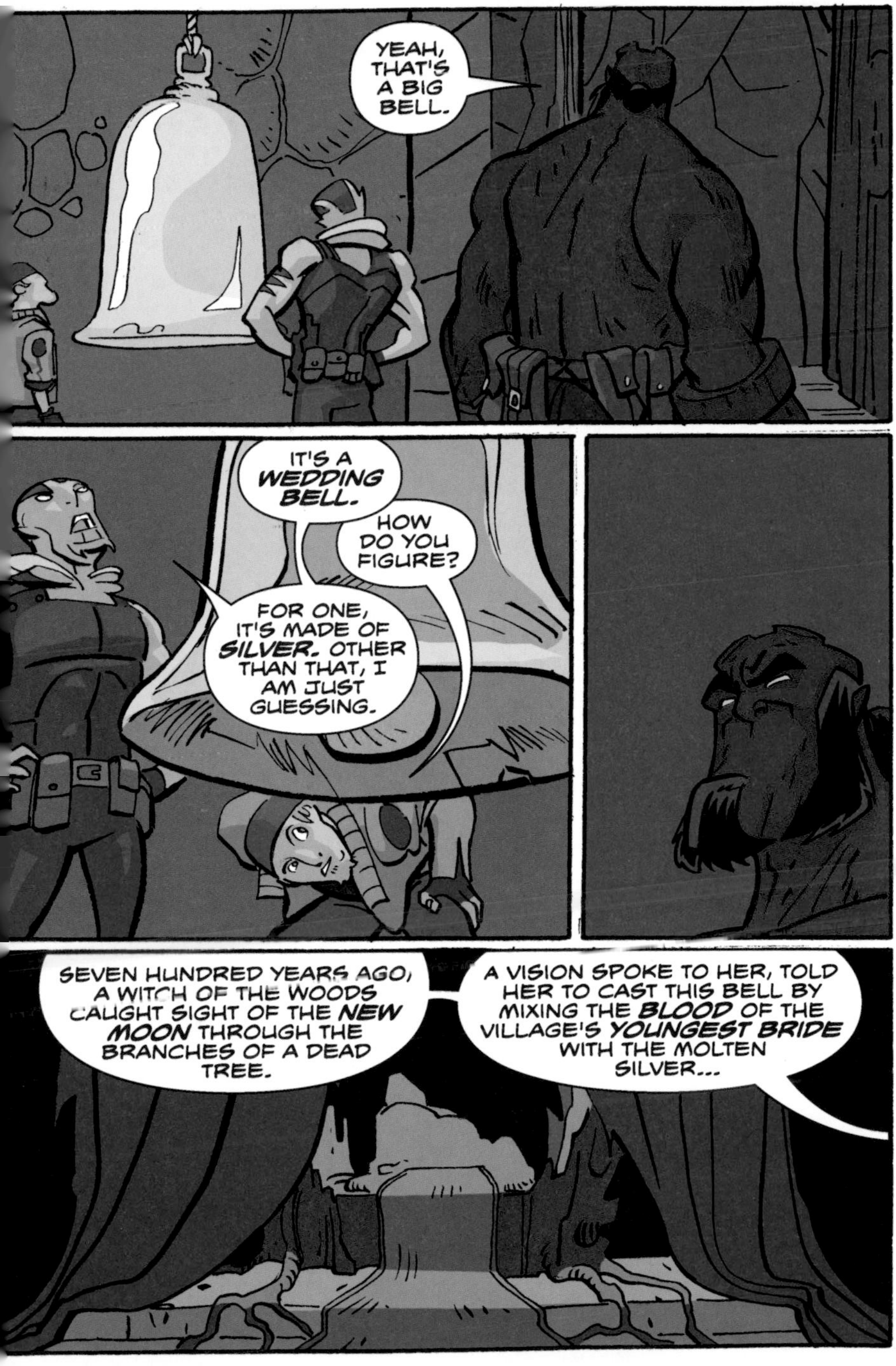
YEAH, THAT'S A BIG BELL.
IT'S A *WEDDING BELL.*
HOW DO YOU FIGURE?
FOR ONE, IT'S MADE OF *SILVER.* OTHER THAN THAT, I AM JUST GUESSING.
SEVEN HUNDRED YEARS AGO, A WITCH OF THE WOODS CAUGHT SIGHT OF THE *NEW MOON* THROUGH THE BRANCHES OF A DEAD TREE.
A VISION SPOKE TO HER, TOLD HER TO CAST THIS BELL BY MIXING THE *BLOOD* OF THE VILLAGE'S *YOUNGEST BRIDE* WITH THE MOLTEN SILVER...

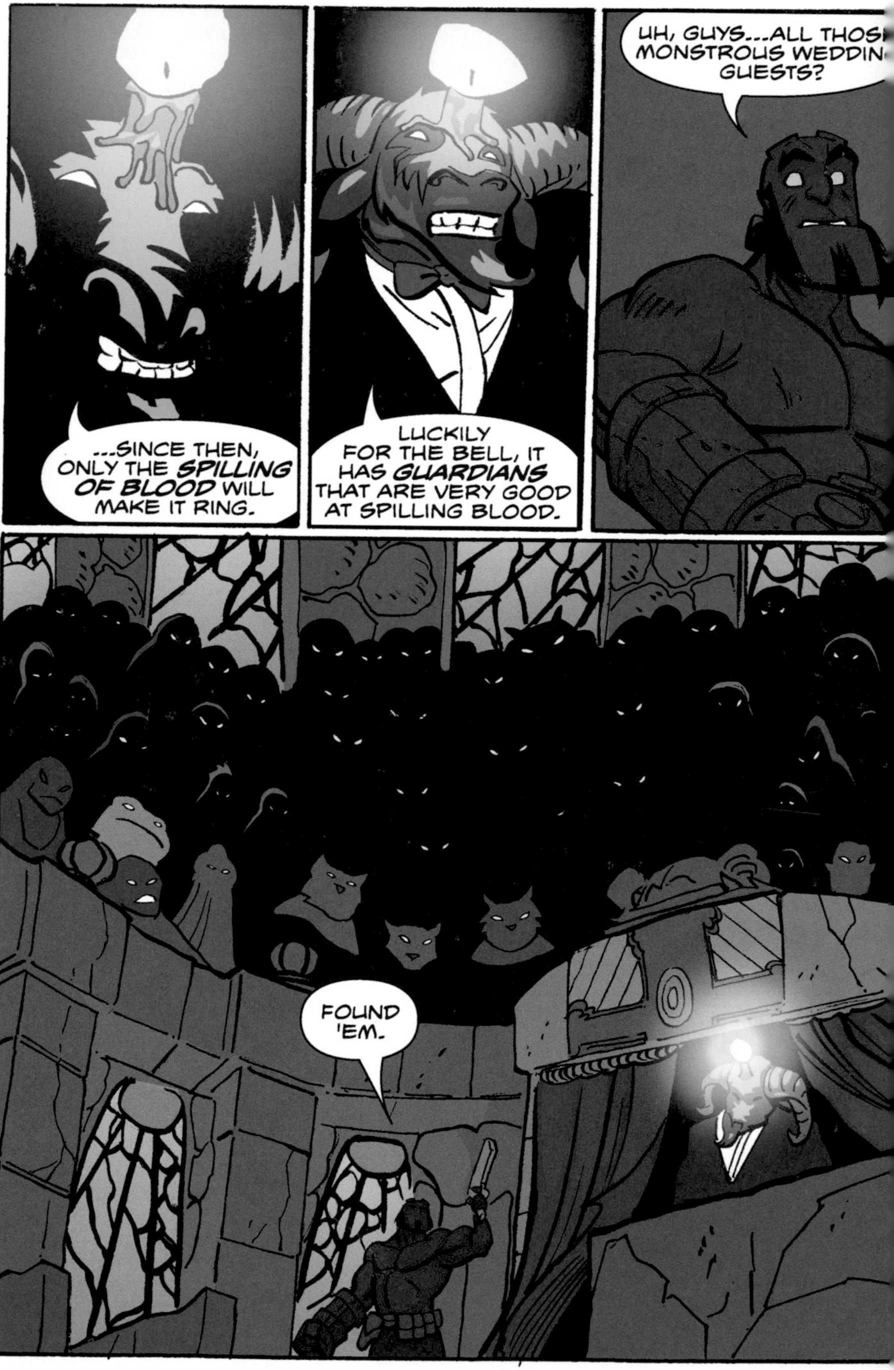
...SINCE THEN, ONLY THE SPILLING OF BLOOD WILL MAKE IT RING.
LUCKILY FOR THE BELL, IT HAS GUARDIANS THAT ARE VERY GOOD AT SPILLING BLOOD.
UH, GUYS...ALL THOS MONSTROUS WEDDIN GUESTS?
FOUND 'EM.

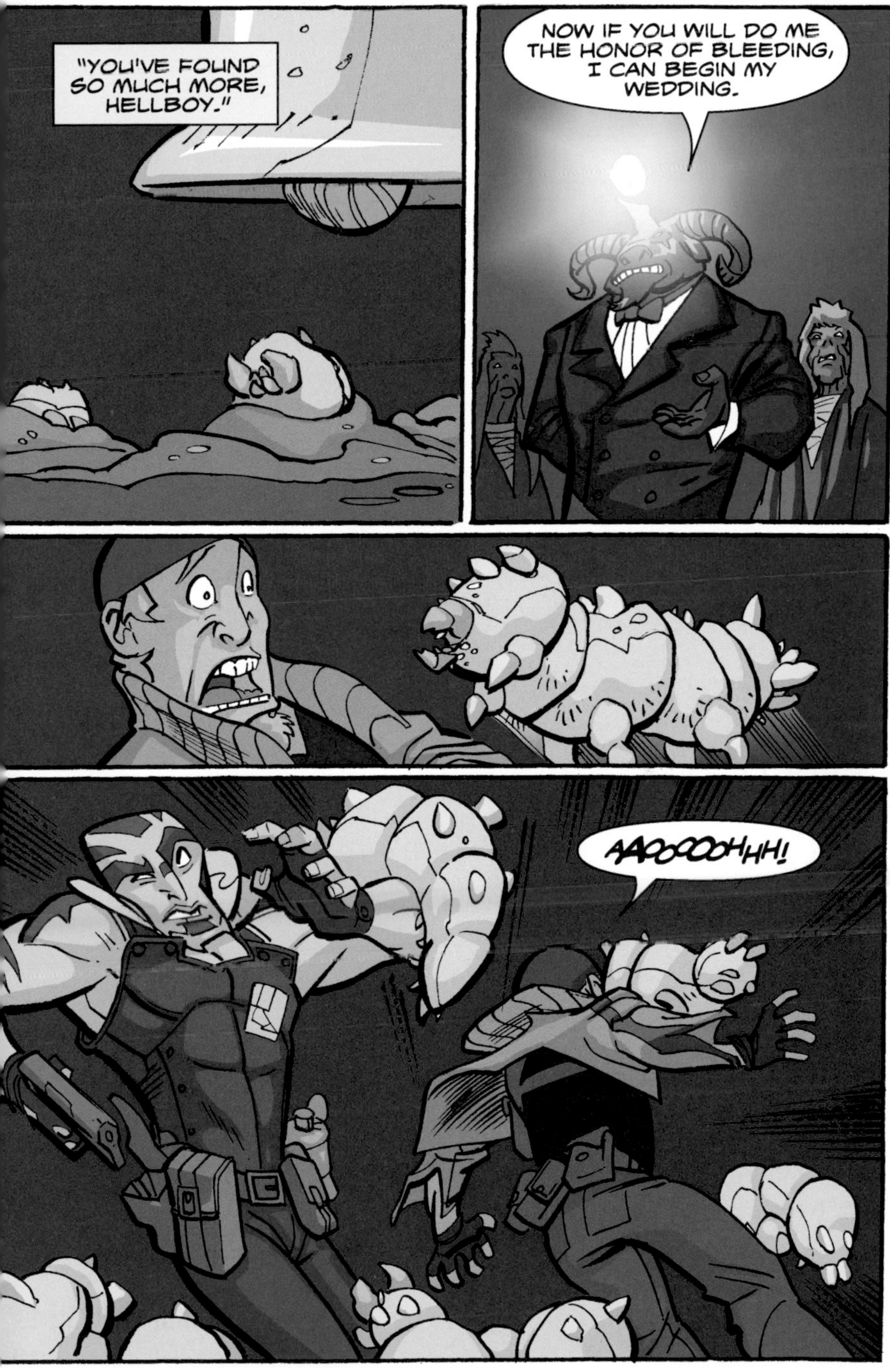
"YOU'VE FOUND SO MUCH MORE, HELLBOY."
NOW IF YOU WILL DO ME THE HONOR OF BLEEDING, I CAN BEGIN MY WEDDING.
AAAOOOOHHH!

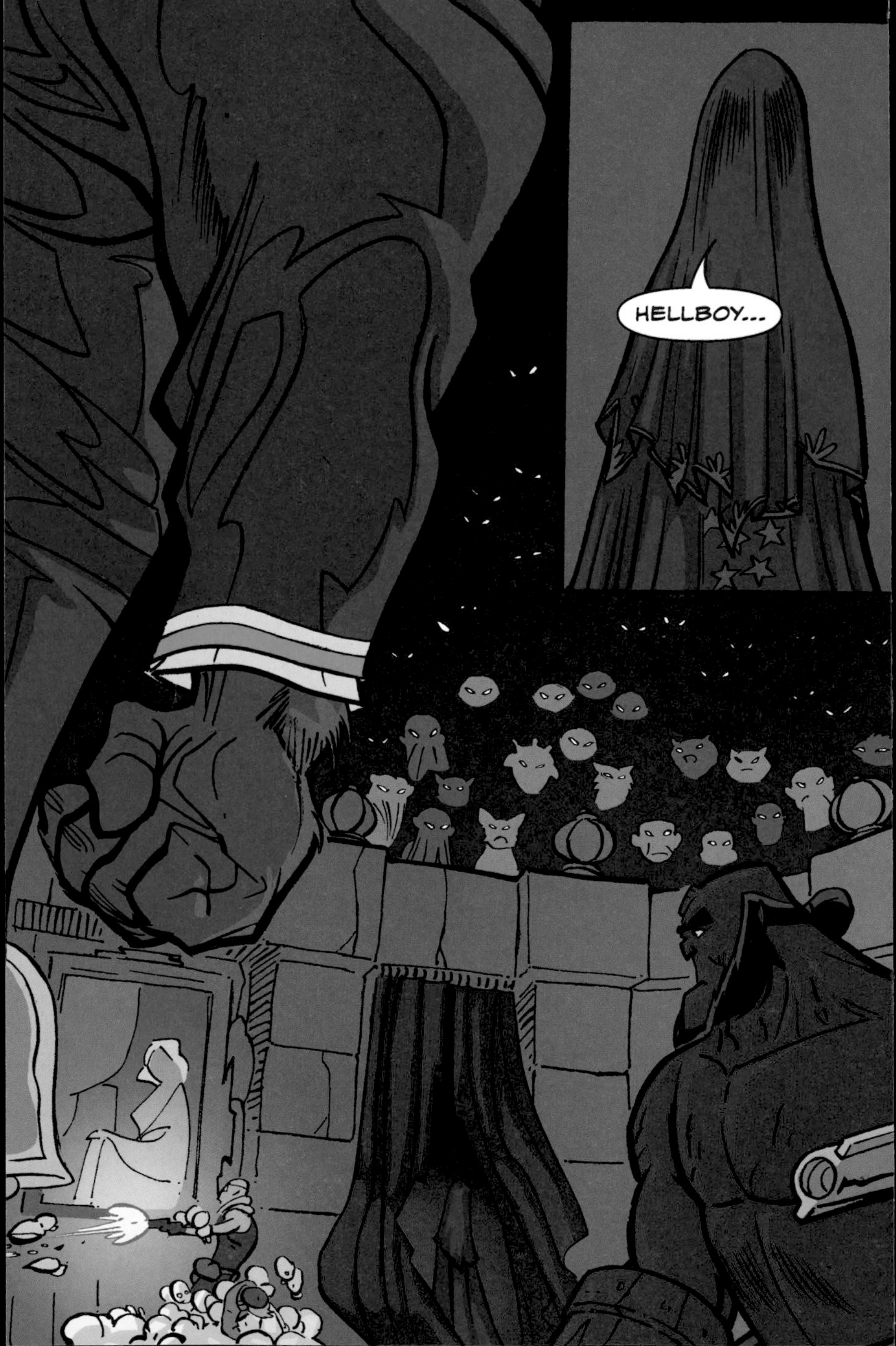
HELLBOY...

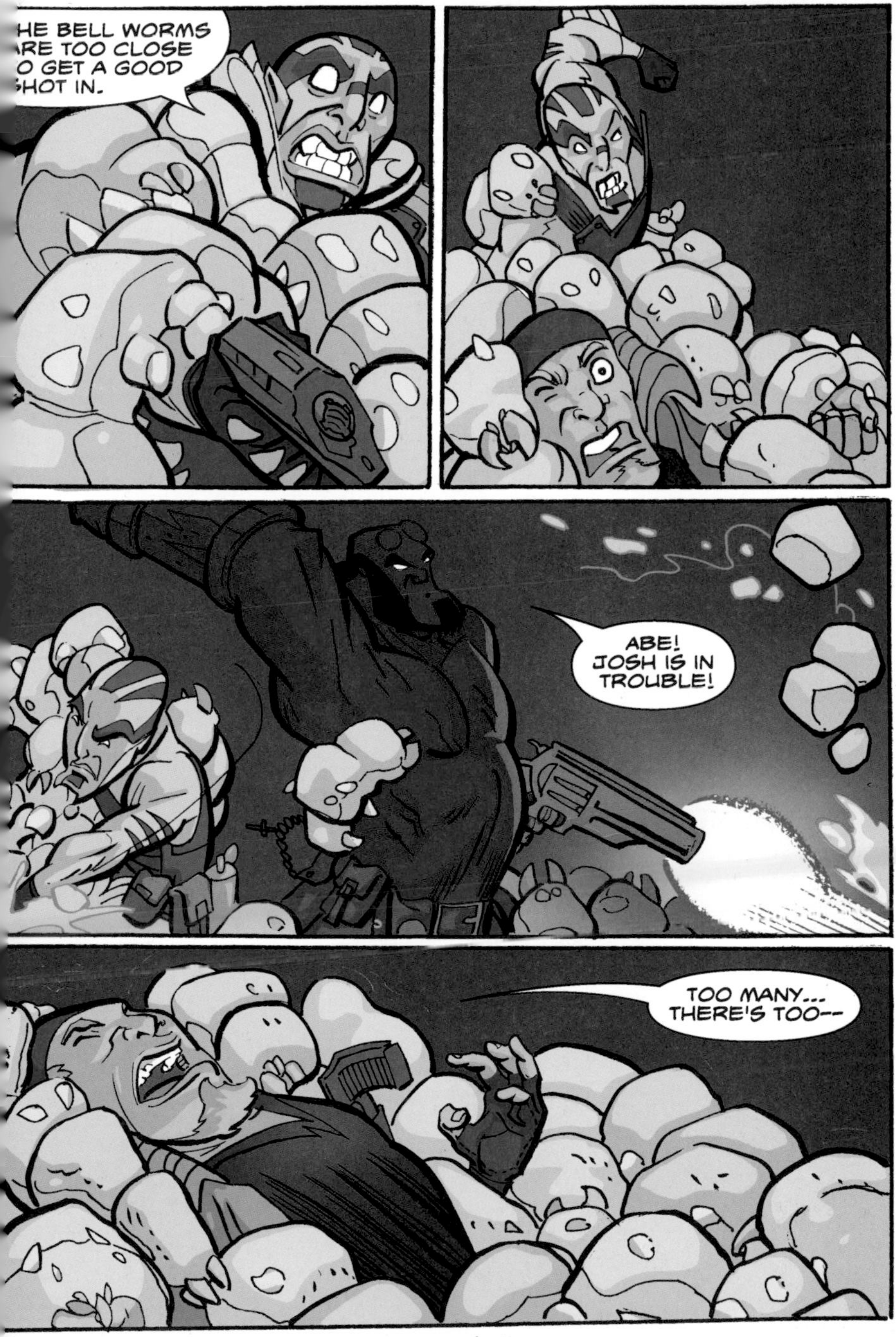
HE BELL WORMS RE TOO CLOSE O GET A GOOD SHOT IN.
ABE! JOSH IS IN TROUBLE!
TOO MANY... THERE'S TOO--

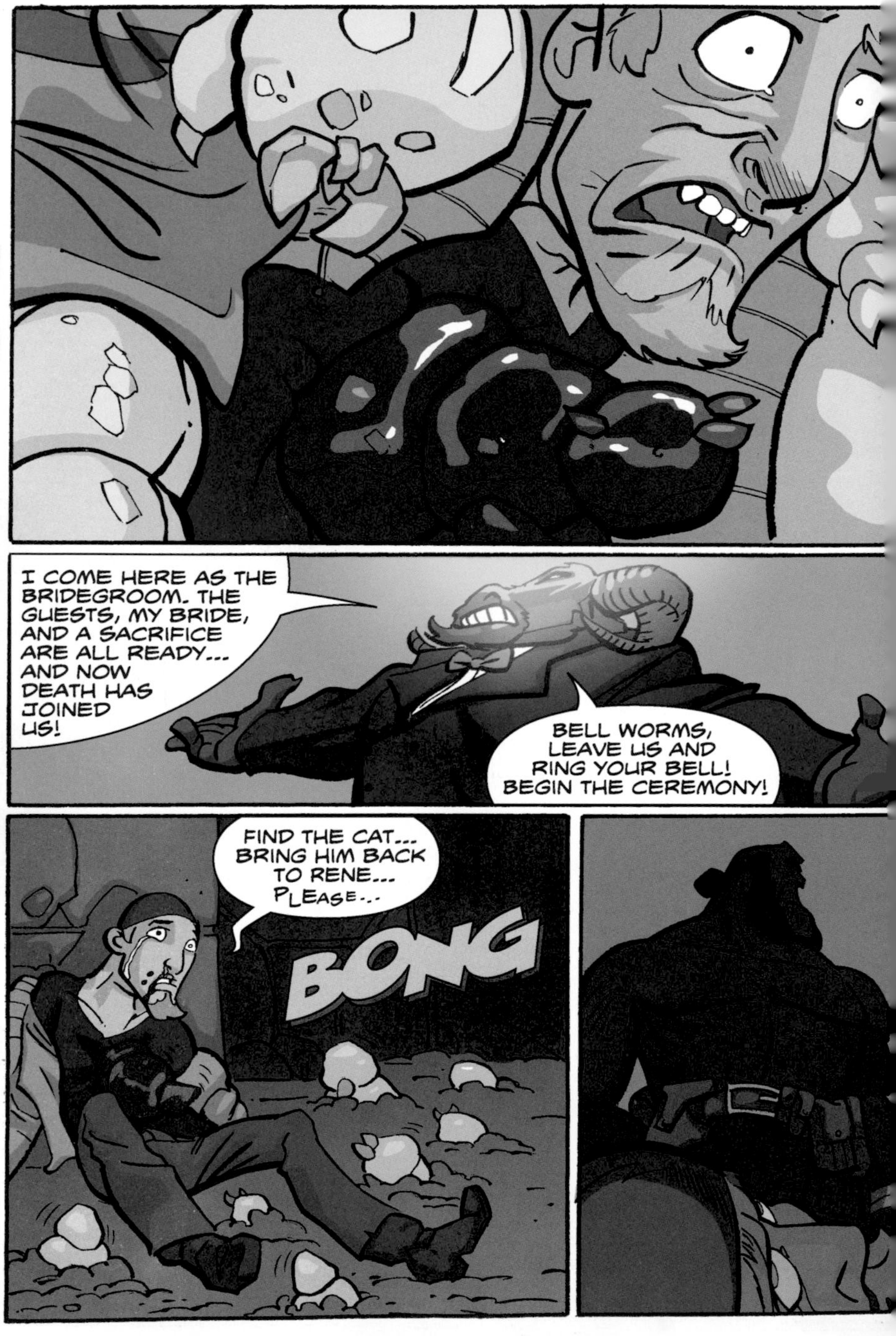
I COME HERE AS THE BRIDEGROOM. THE GUESTS, MY BRIDE, AND A SACRIFICE ARE ALL READY... AND NOW DEATH HAS JOINED US!
BELL WORMS, LEAVE US AND RING YOUR BELL! BEGIN THE CEREMONY!
FIND THE CAT... BRING HIM BACK TO RENE... PLEASE...
BONG

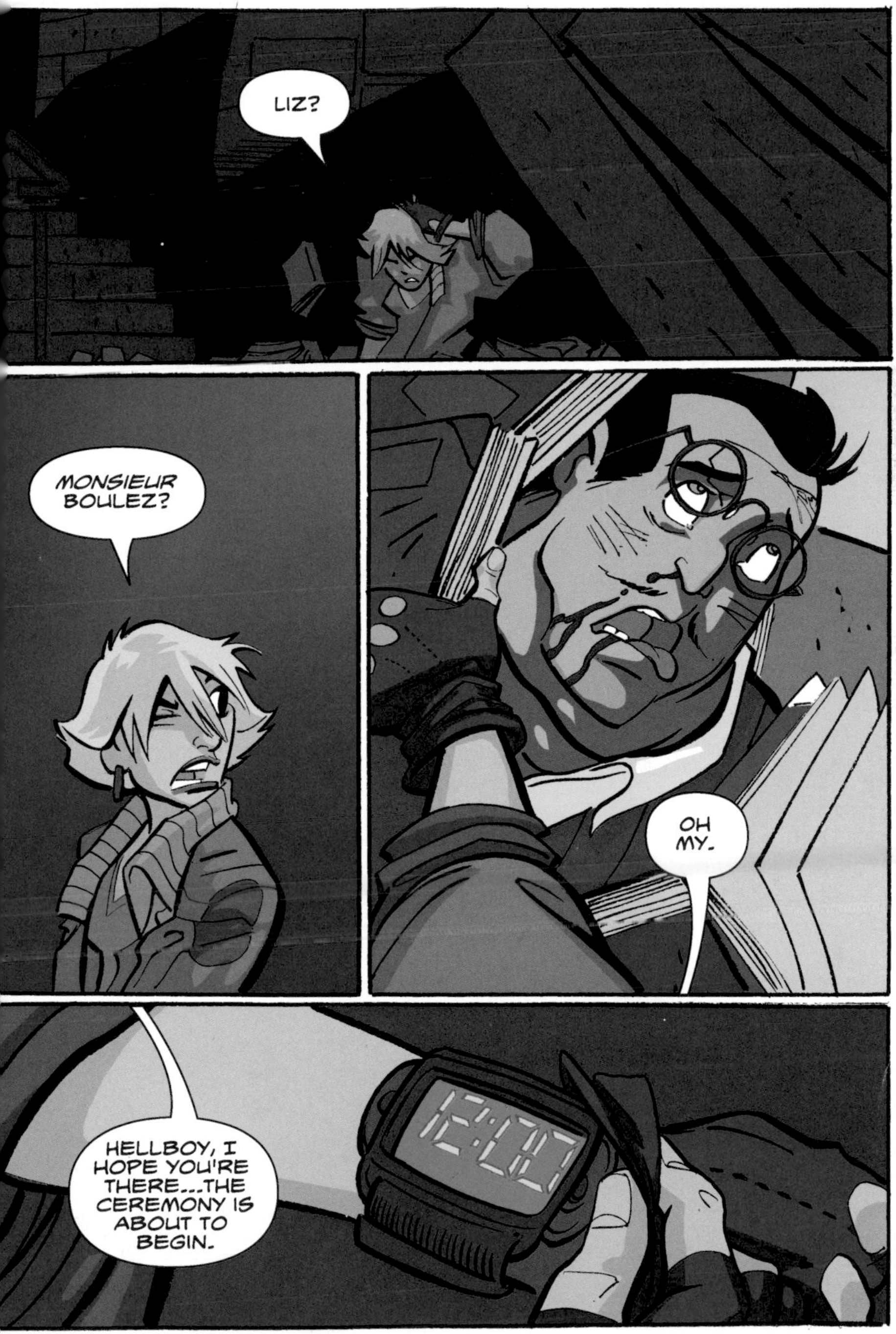
LIZ?
MONSIEUR BOULEZ?
OH MY.
HELLBOY, I HOPE YOU'RE THERE...THE CEREMONY IS ABOUT TO BEGIN.

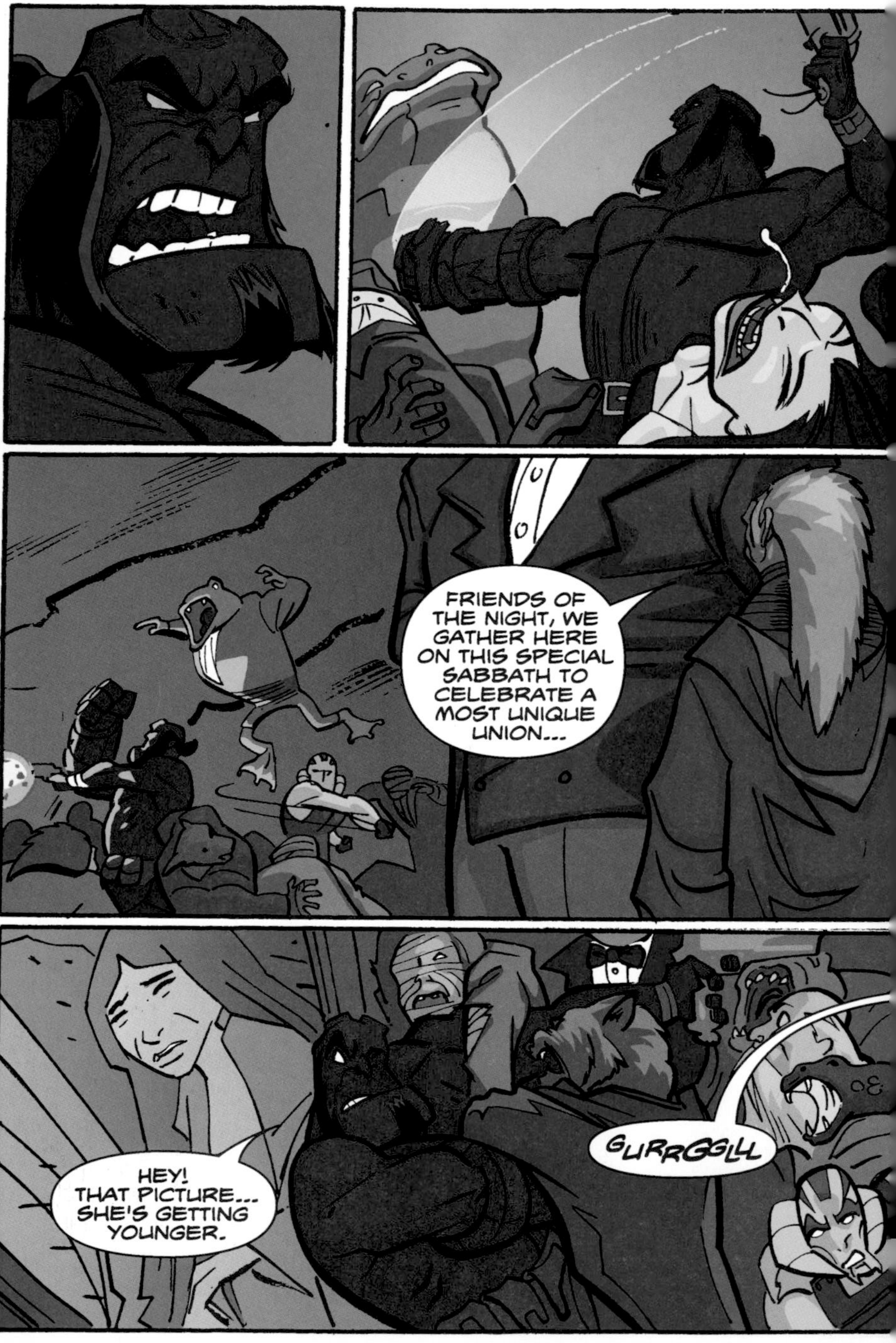
FRIENDS OF THE NIGHT, WE GATHER HERE ON THIS SPECIAL SABBATH TO CELEBRATE A MOST UNIQUE UNION...
HEY! THAT PICTURE... SHE'S GETTING YOUNGER.
GURRGGLLL

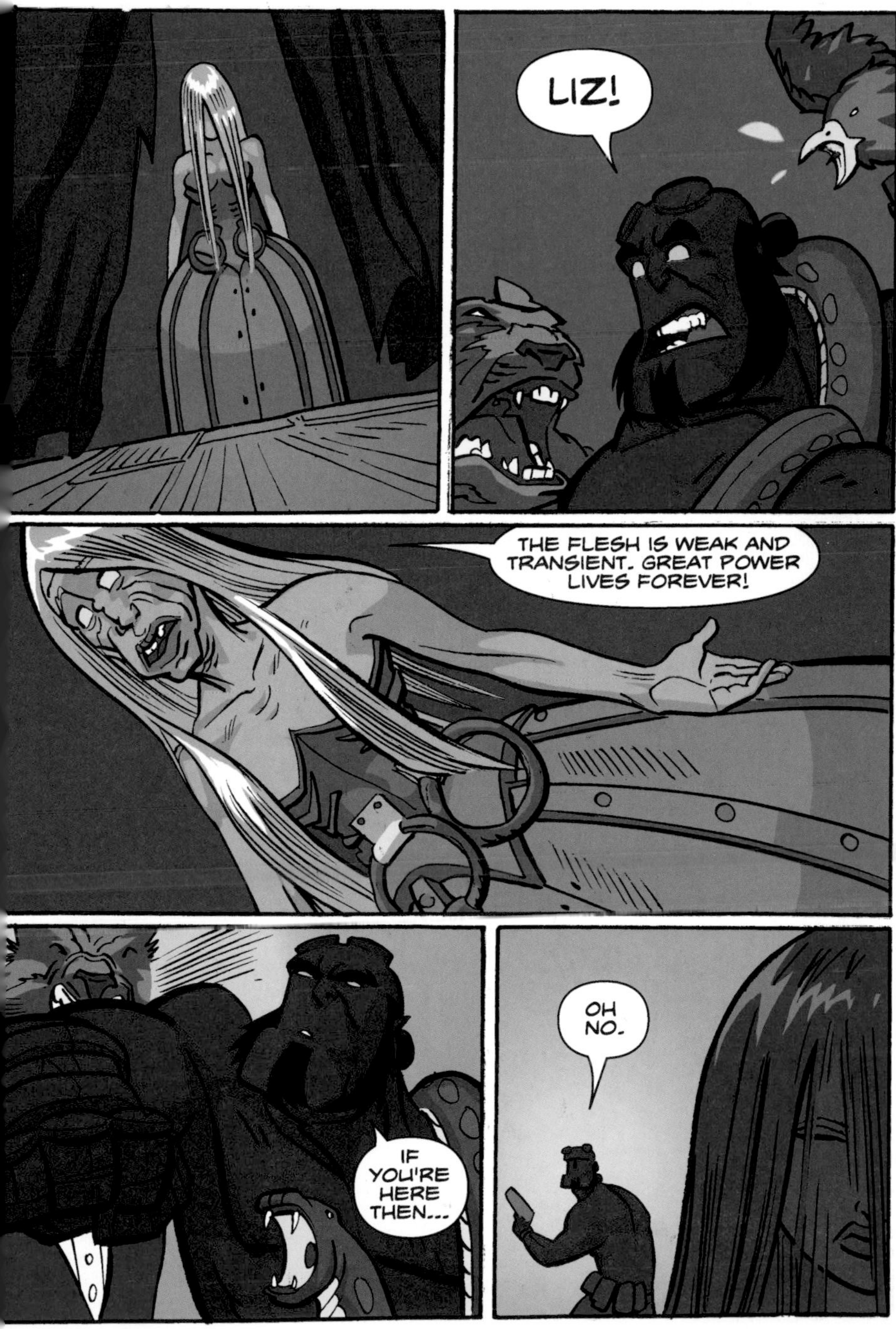
LIZ!
THE FLESH IS WEAK AND TRANSIENT. GREAT POWER LIVES FOREVER!
IF YOU'RE HERE THEN...
OH NO.

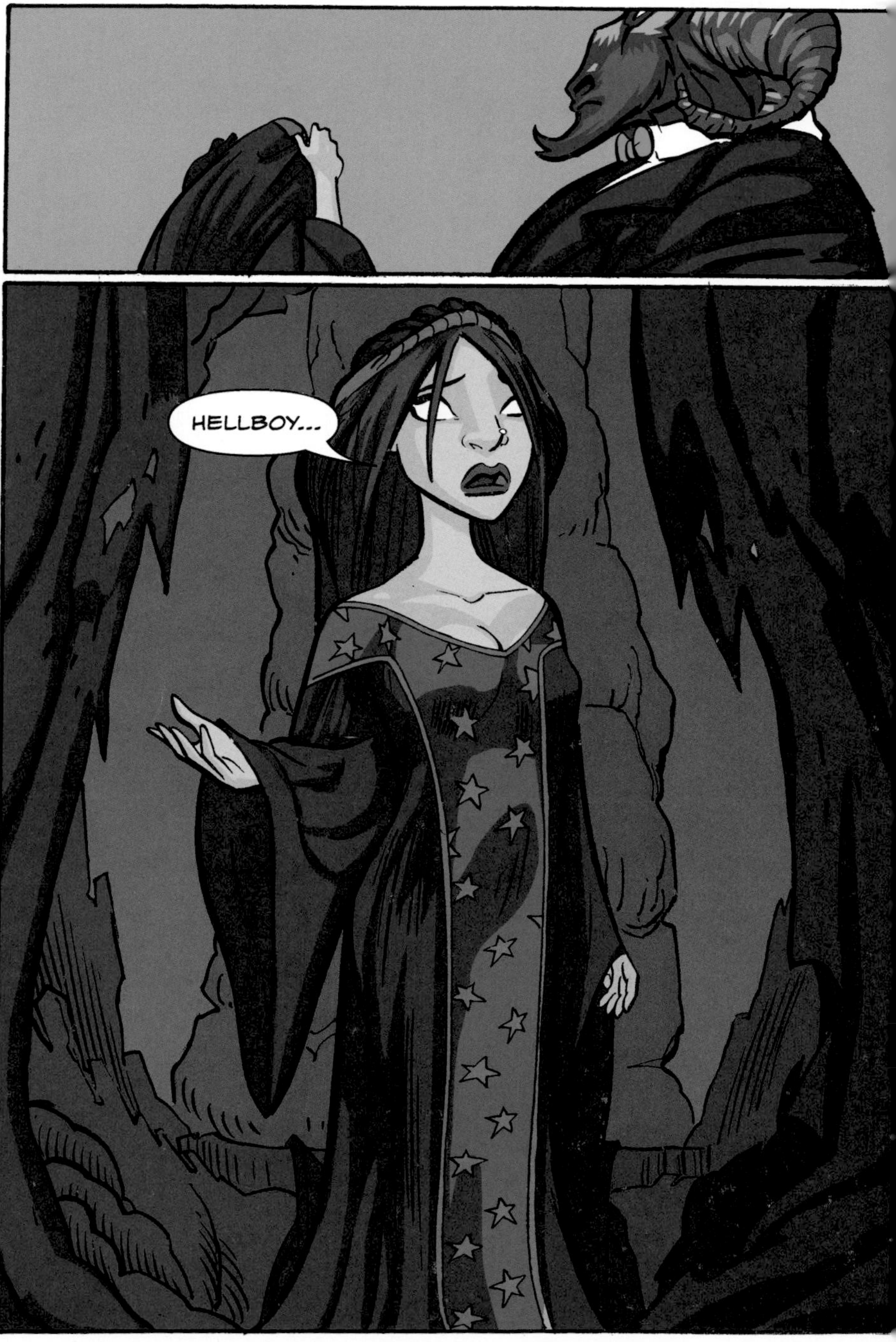
HELLBOY...

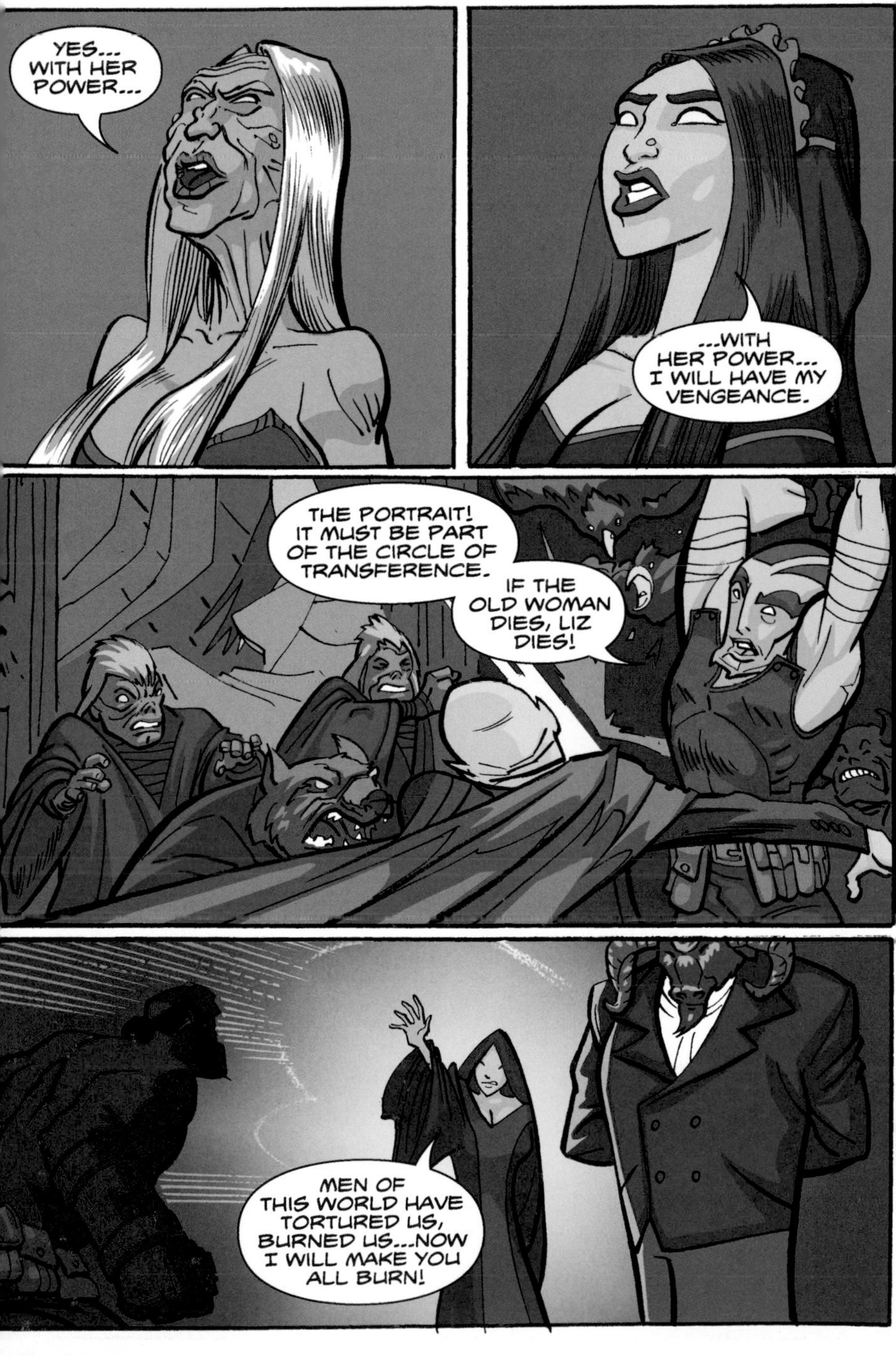
YES... WITH HER POWER...
...WITH HER POWER... I WILL HAVE MY VENGEANCE.
THE PORTRAIT! IT MUST BE PART OF THE CIRCLE OF TRANSFERENCE.
IF THE OLD WOMAN DIES, LIZ DIES!
MEN OF THIS WORLD HAVE TORTURED US, BURNED US...NOW I WILL MAKE YOU ALL BURN!

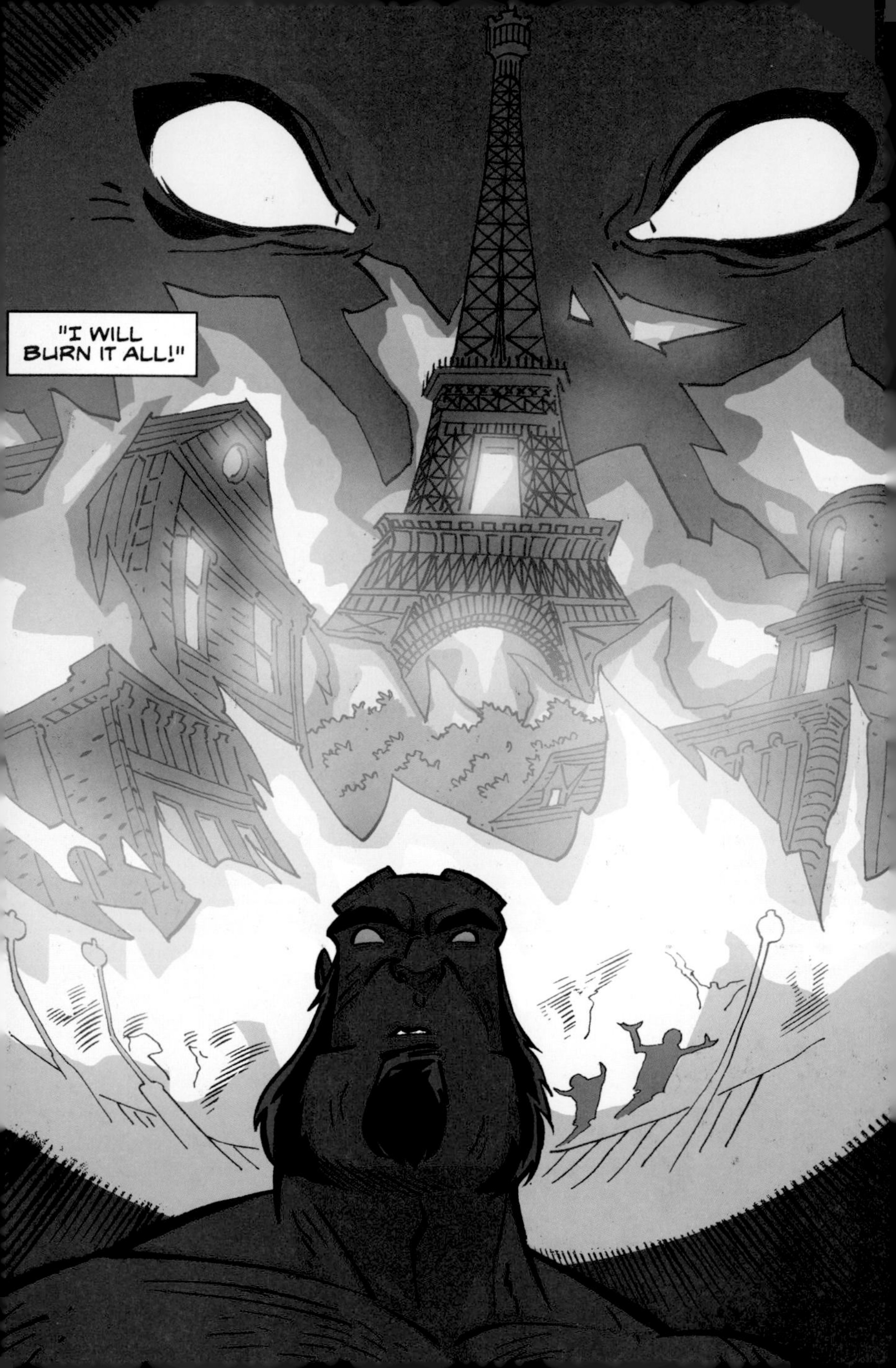
"I WILL BURN IT ALL!"

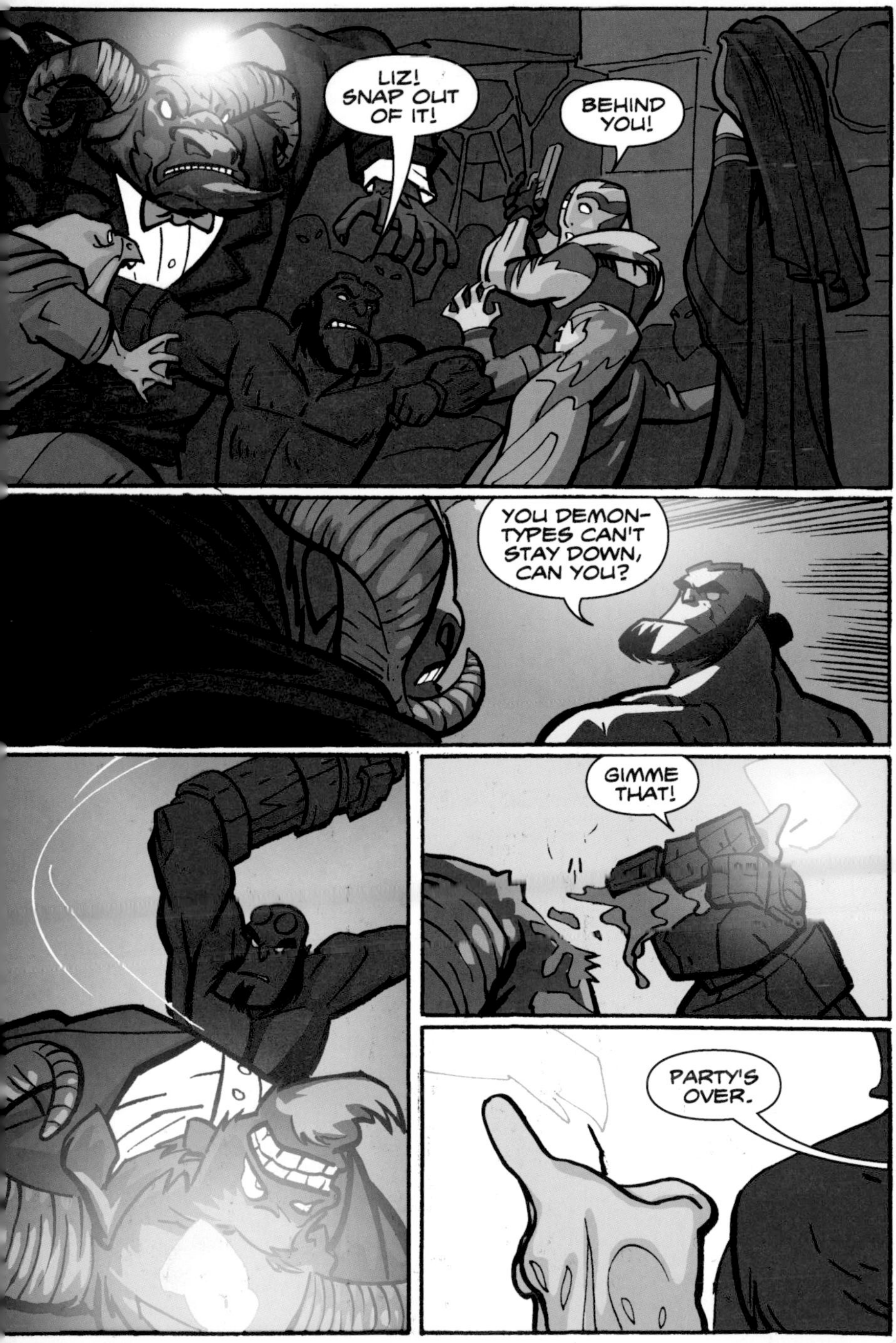
LIZ! SNAP OUT OF IT!
BEHIND YOU!
YOU DEMON-TYPES CAN'T STAY DOWN, CAN YOU?
GIMME THAT!
PARTY'S OVER.

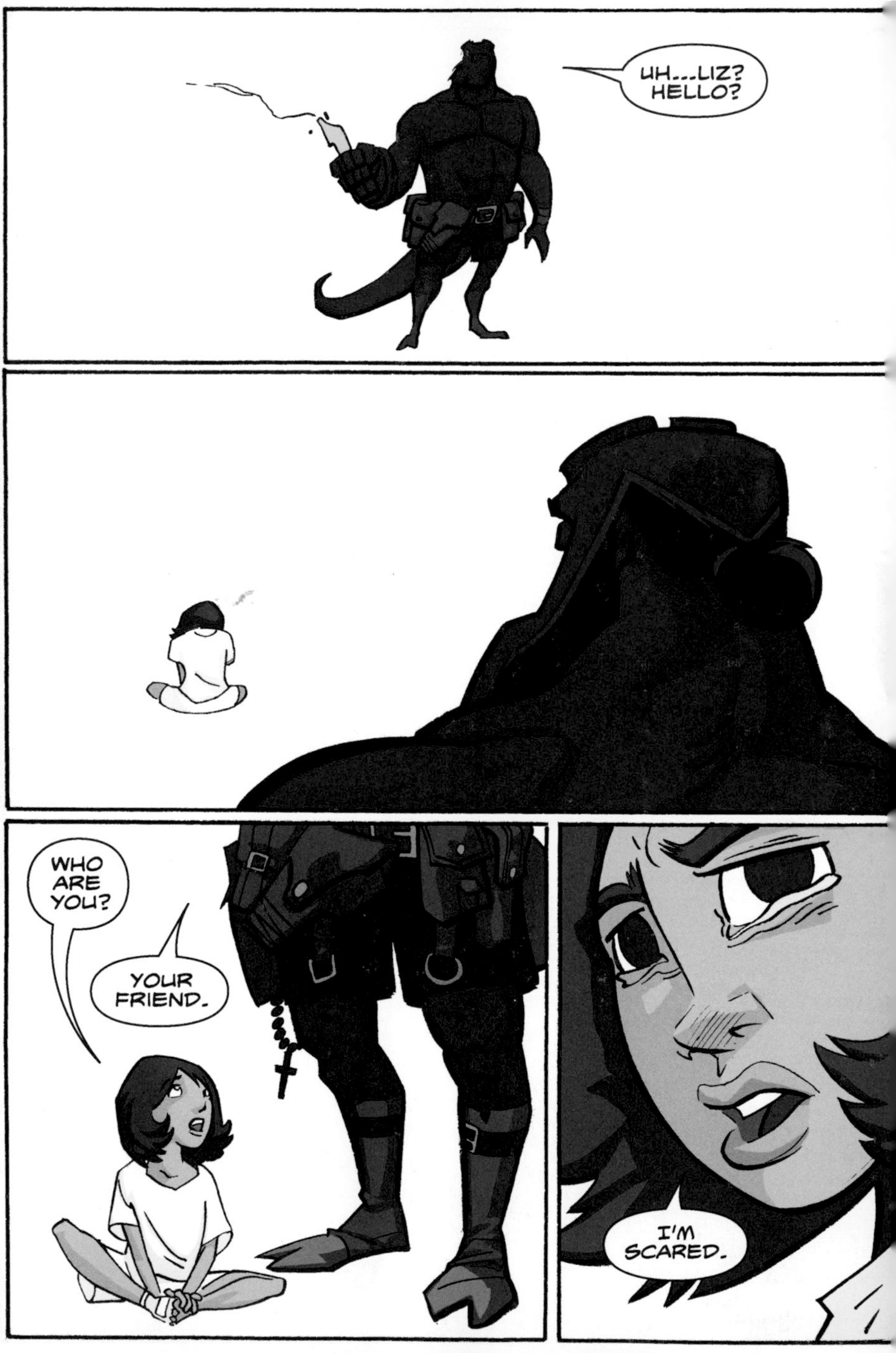
UH...LIZ? HELLO?
WHO ARE YOU?
YOUR FRIEND.
I'M SCARED.

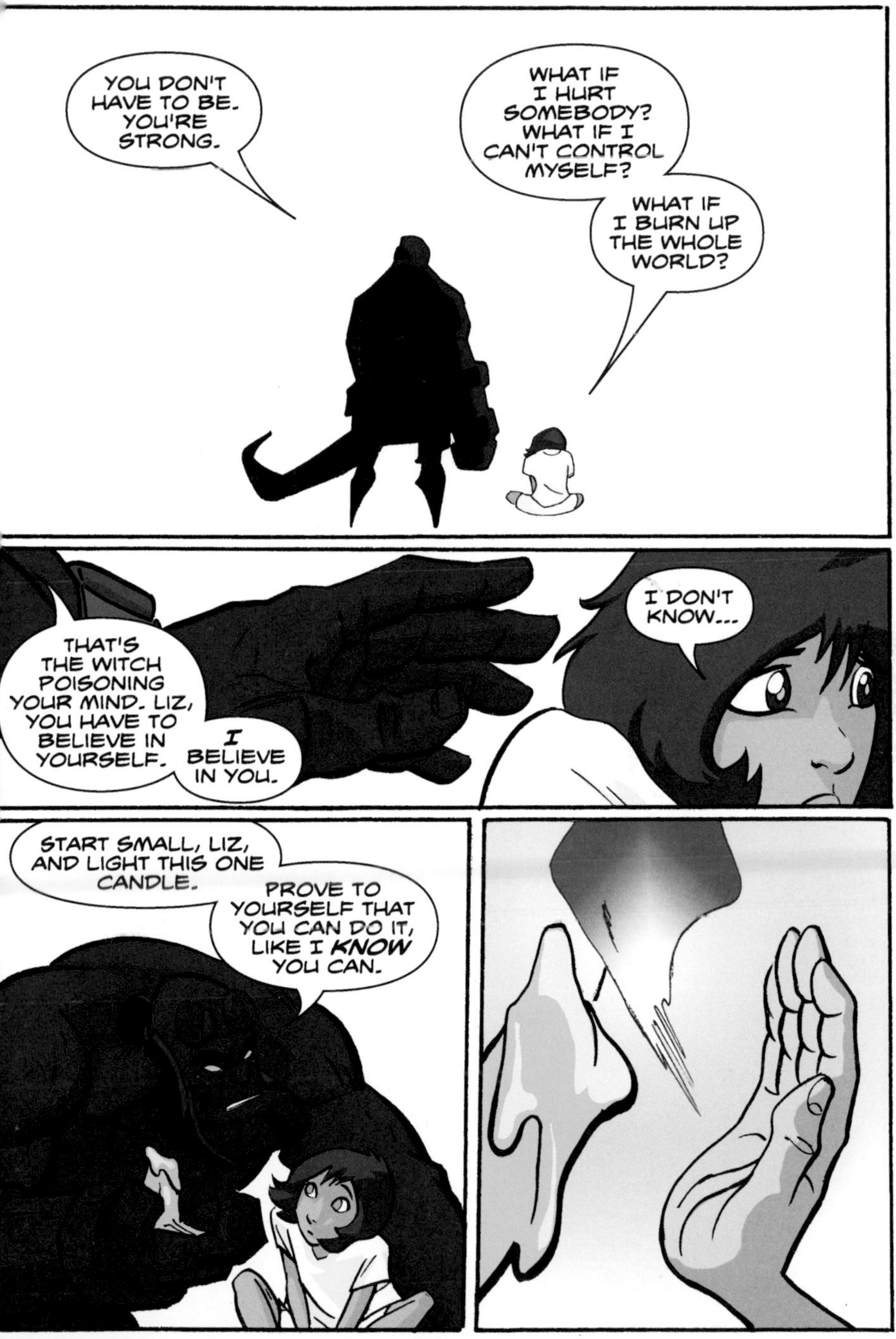
YOU DON'T HAVE TO BE. YOU'RE STRONG.
WHAT IF I HURT SOMEBODY? WHAT IF I CAN'T CONTROL MYSELF?
WHAT IF I BURN UP THE WHOLE WORLD?
I DON'T KNOW...
THAT'S THE WITCH POISONING YOUR MIND. LIZ, YOU HAVE TO BELIEVE IN YOURSELF.
I BELIEVE IN YOU.
START SMALL, LIZ, AND LIGHT THIS ONE CANDLE.
PROVE TO YOURSELF THAT YOU CAN DO IT, LIKE I *KNOW* YOU CAN.

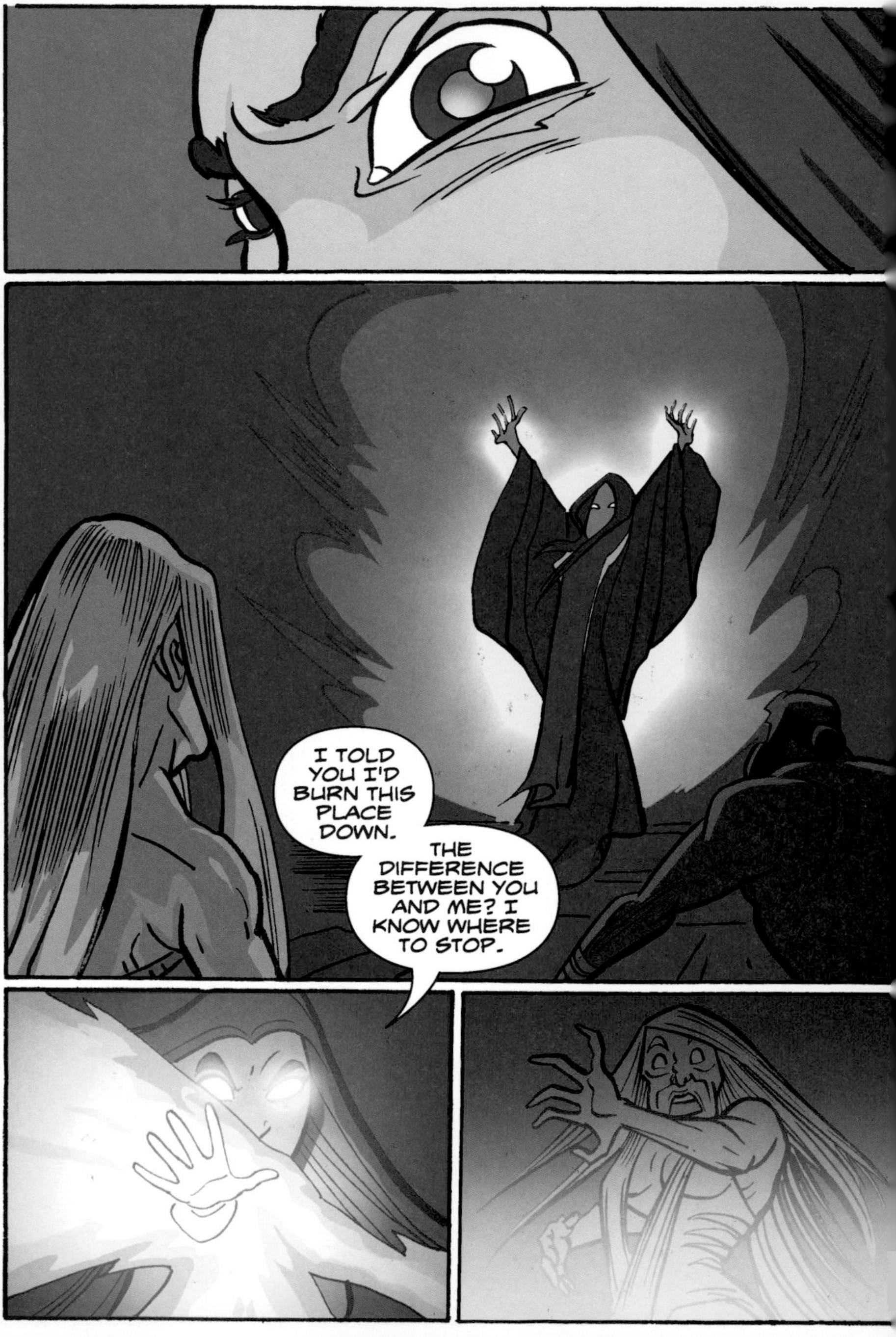
I TOLD YOU I'D BURN THIS PLACE DOWN.
THE DIFFERENCE BETWEEN YOU AND ME? I KNOW WHERE TO STOP.

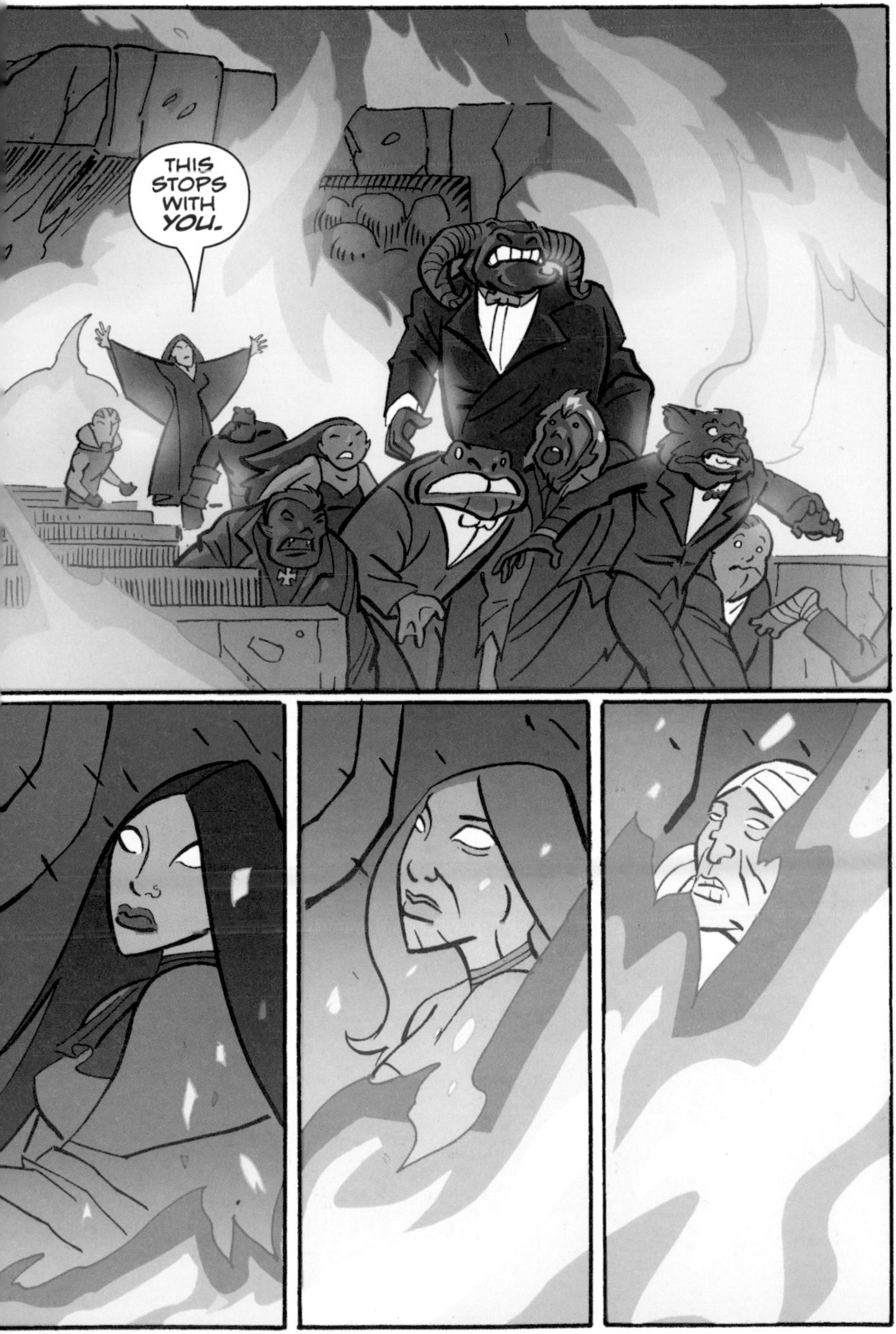
THIS STOPS WITH *YOU*.

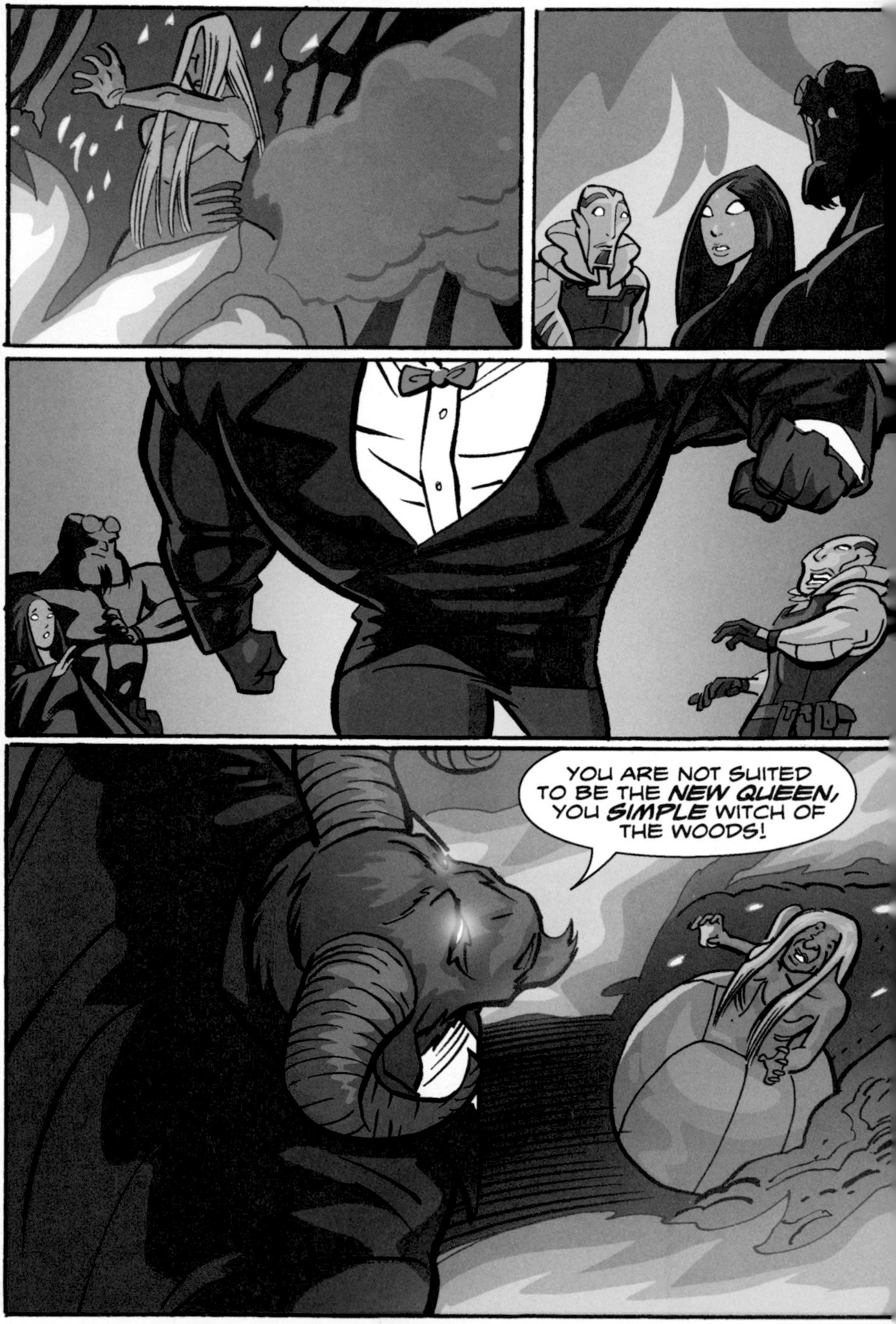
YOU ARE NOT SUITED TO BE THE NEW QUEEN, YOU SIMPLE WITCH OF THE WOODS!

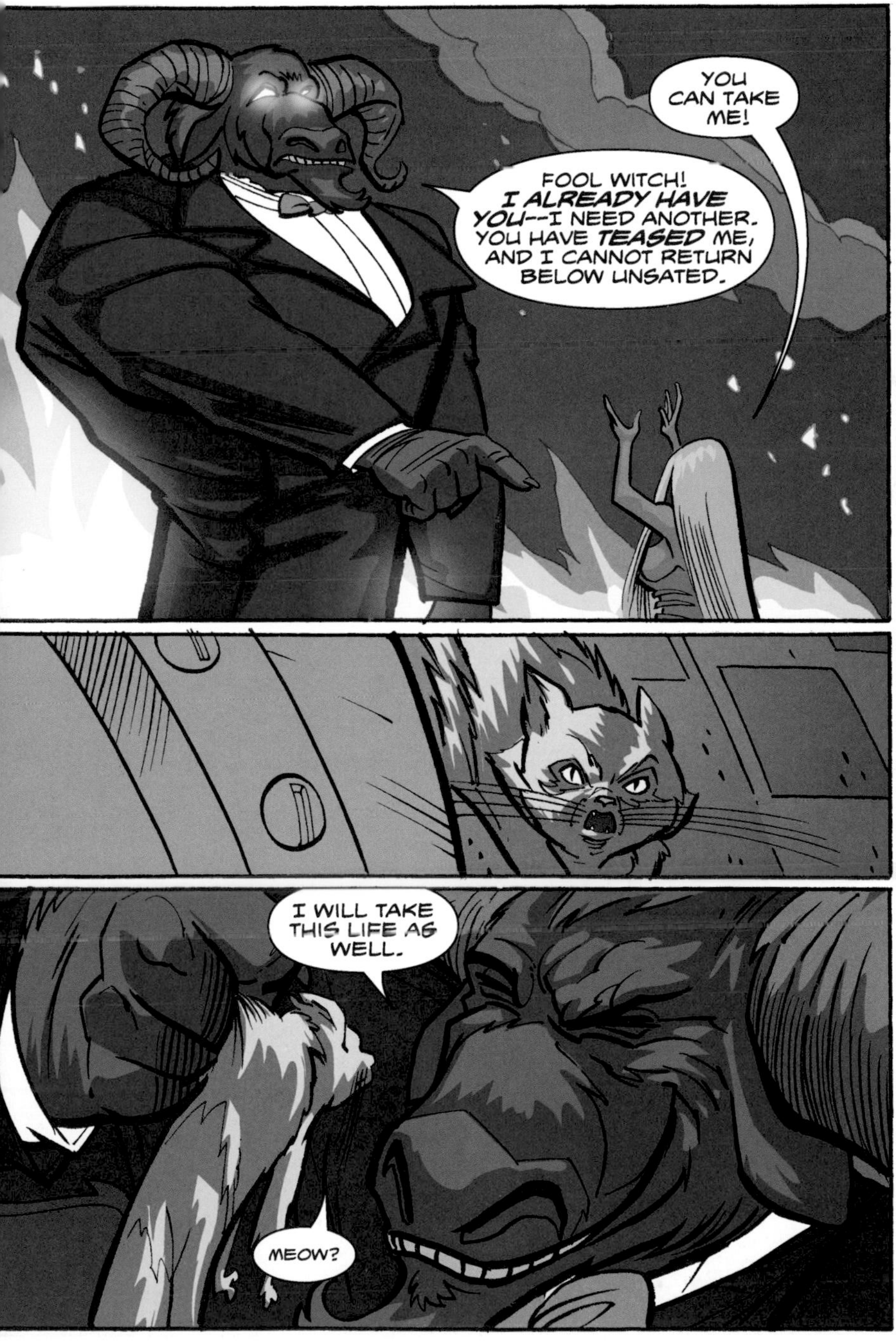
YOU CAN TAKE ME!
FOOL WITCH! I ALREADY HAVE YOU--I NEED ANOTHER. YOU HAVE TEASED ME, AND I CANNOT RETURN BELOW UNSATED.
I WILL TAKE THIS LIFE AS WELL.
MEOW?

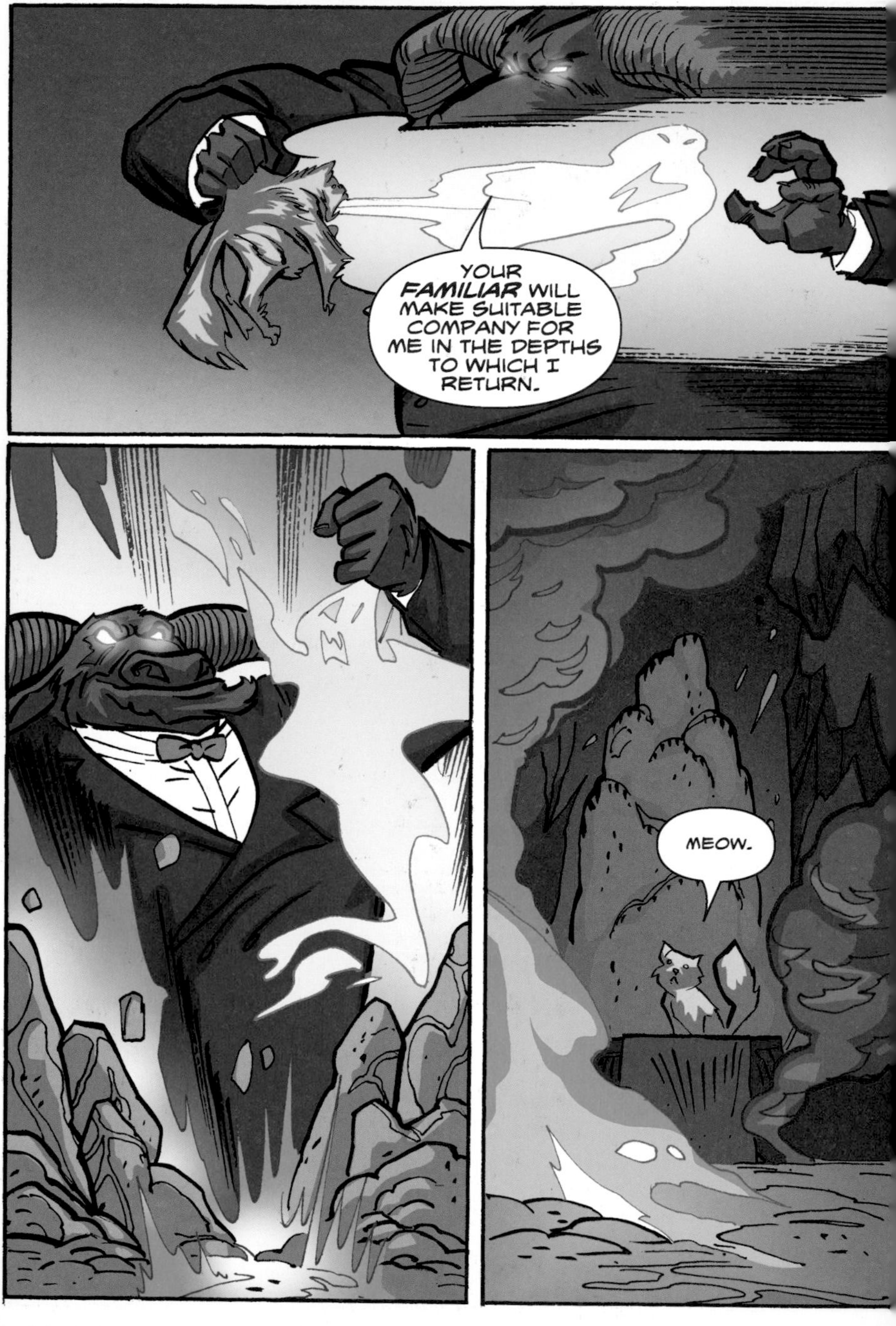
YOUR FAMILIAR WILL MAKE SUITABLE COMPANY FOR ME IN THE DEPTHS TO WHICH I RETURN.
MEOW.

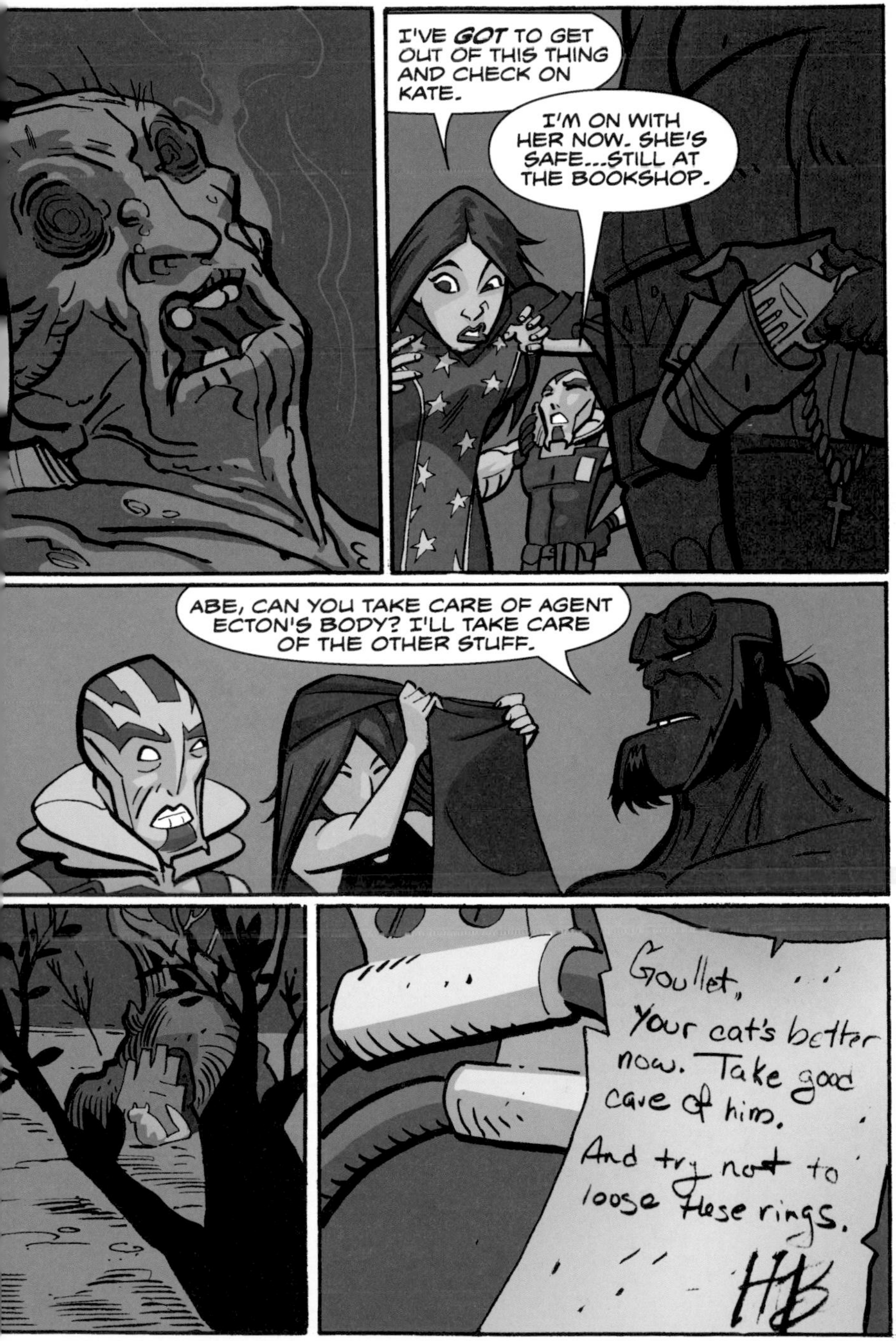
I'VE GOT TO GET OUT OF THIS THING AND CHECK ON KATE.
I'M ON WITH HER NOW. SHE'S SAFE...STILL AT THE BOOKSHOP.
ABE, CAN YOU TAKE CARE OF AGENT ECTON'S BODY? I'LL TAKE CARE OF THE OTHER STUFF.
Goullet,
Your cat's better now. Take good care of him.
And try not to loose these rings.
HB

THE END

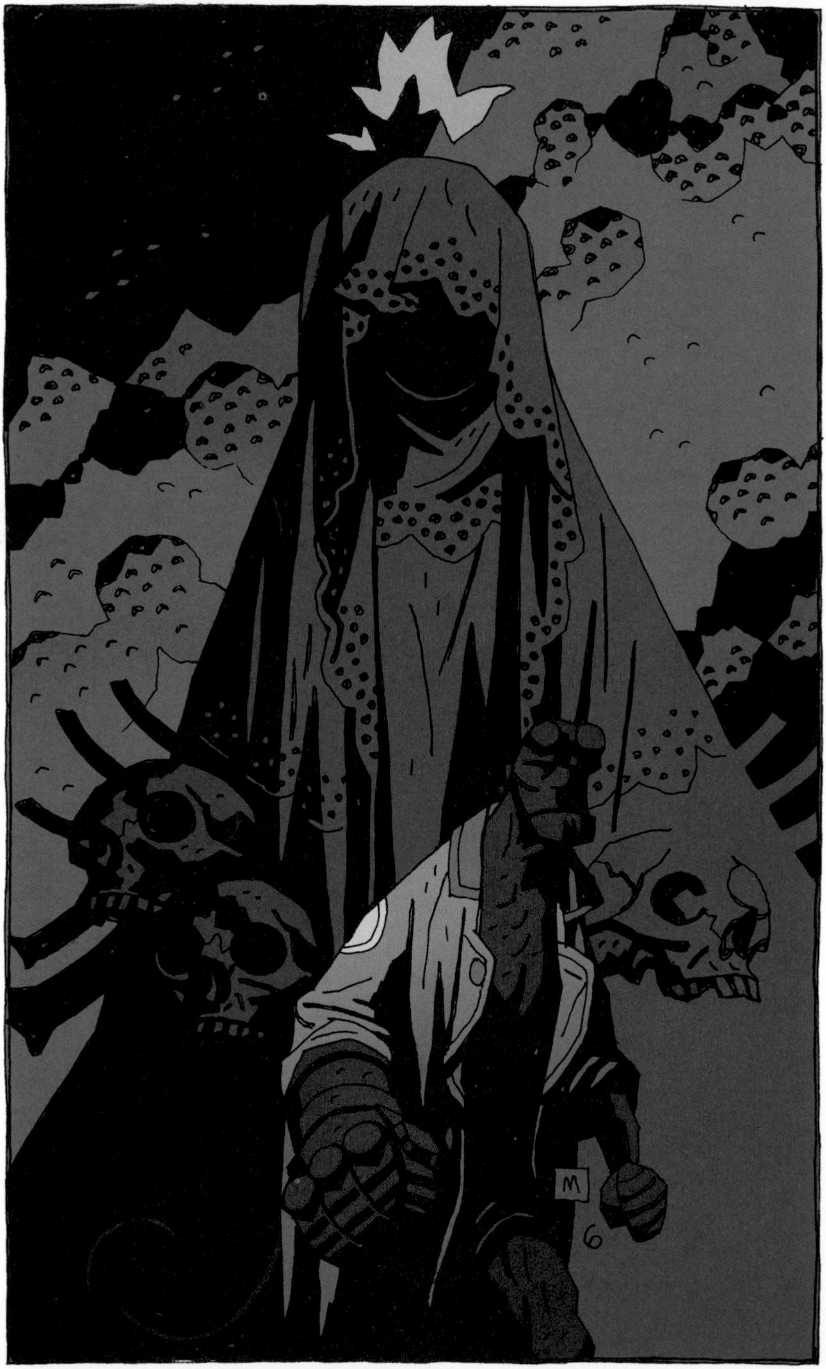

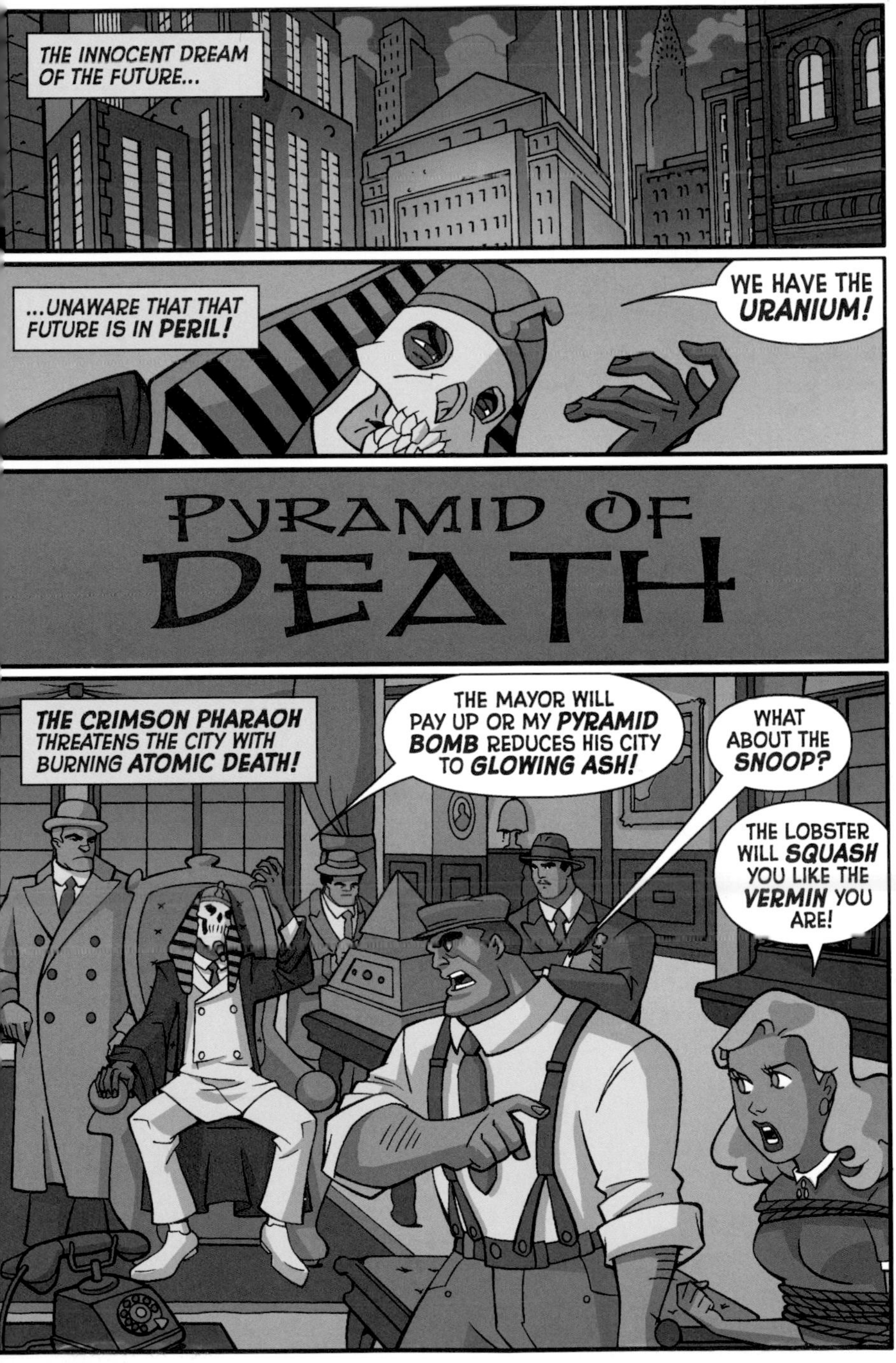
THE INNOCENT DREAM OF THE FUTURE...
...UNAWARE THAT THAT FUTURE IS IN PERIL!
WE HAVE THE URANIUM!
PYRAMID OF DEATH
THE CRIMSON PHARAOH THREATENS THE CITY WITH BURNING ATOMIC DEATH!
THE MAYOR WILL PAY UP OR MY PYRAMID BOMB REDUCES HIS CITY TO GLOWING ASH!
WHAT ABOUT THE SNOOP?
THE LOBSTER WILL SQUASH YOU LIKE THE VERMIN YOU ARE!

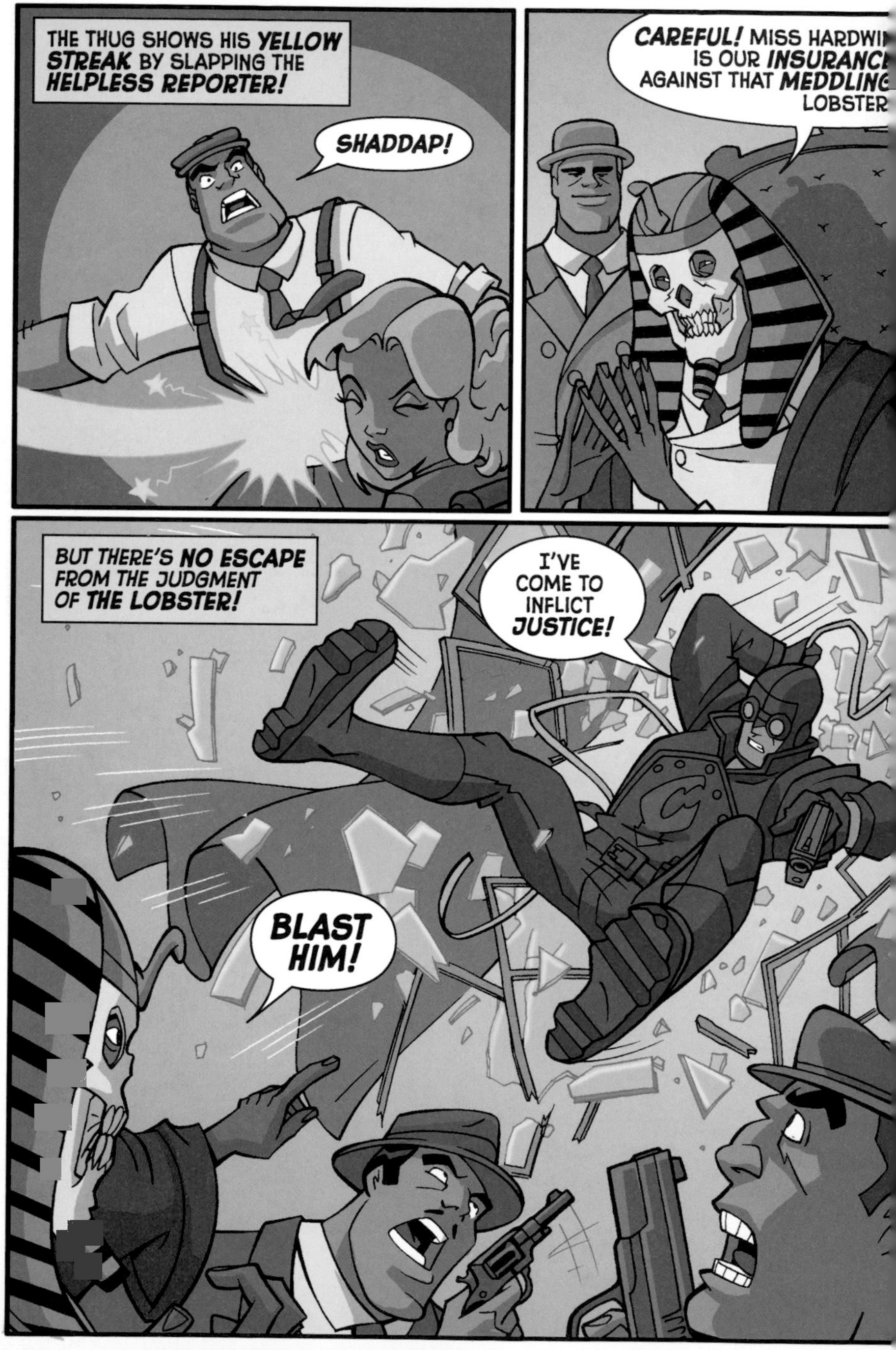
THE THUG SHOWS HIS YELLOW STREAK BY SLAPPING THE HELPLESS REPORTER!
SHADDAP!
CAREFUL! MISS HARDWI IS OUR INSURANC AGAINST THAT MEDDLING LOBSTER
BUT THERE'S NO ESCAPE FROM THE JUDGMENT OF THE LOBSTER!
I'VE COME TO INFLICT JUSTICE!
BLAST HIM!

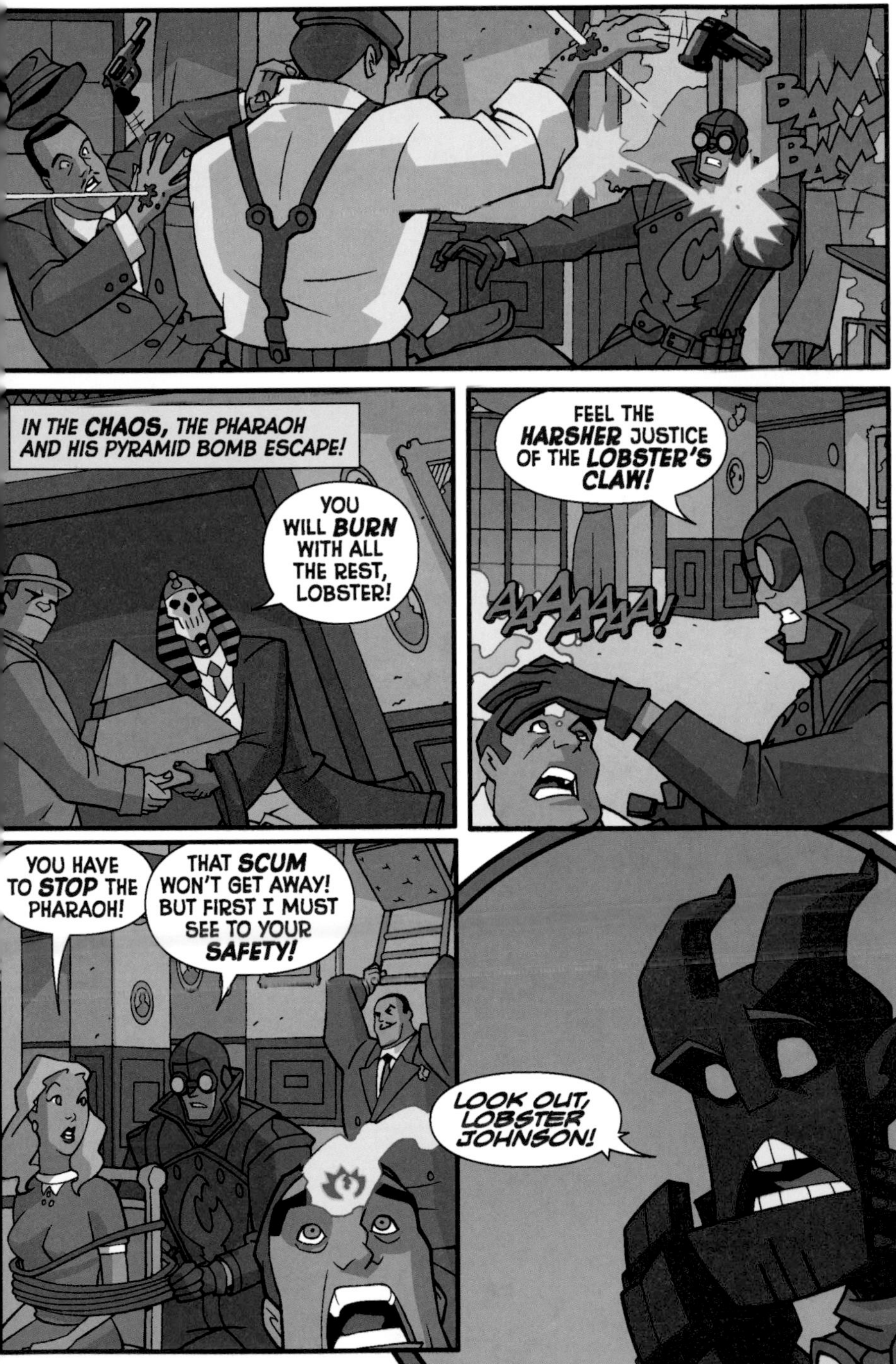
BAM BAM BAM
IN THE CHAOS, THE PHARAOH AND HIS PYRAMID BOMB ESCAPE!
YOU WILL BURN WITH ALL THE REST, LOBSTER!
FEEL THE HARSHER JUSTICE OF THE LOBSTER'S CLAW!
AAAAAAA!
YOU HAVE TO STOP THE PHARAOH!
THAT SCUM WON'T GET AWAY! BUT FIRST I MUST SEE TO YOUR SAFETY!
LOOK OUT, LOBSTER JOHNSON!

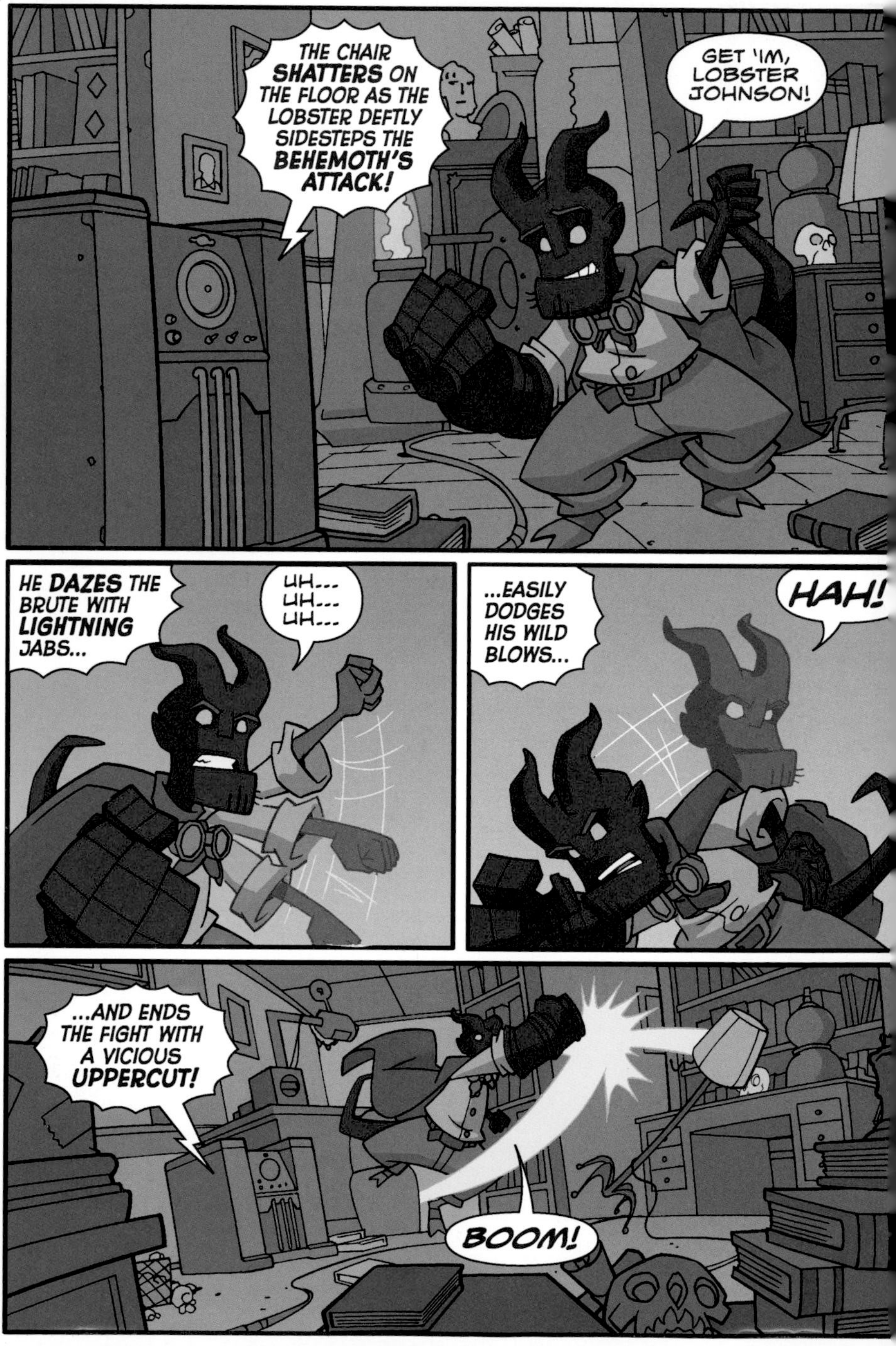
THE CHAIR SHATTERS ON THE FLOOR AS THE LOBSTER DEFTLY SIDESTEPS THE BEHEMOTH'S ATTACK!
GET 'IM, LOBSTER JOHNSON!
HE DAZES THE BRUTE WITH LIGHTNING JABS...
UH--- UH--- UH---
...EASILY DODGES HIS WILD BLOWS...
HAH!
...AND ENDS THE FIGHT WITH A VICIOUS UPPERCUT!
BOOM!

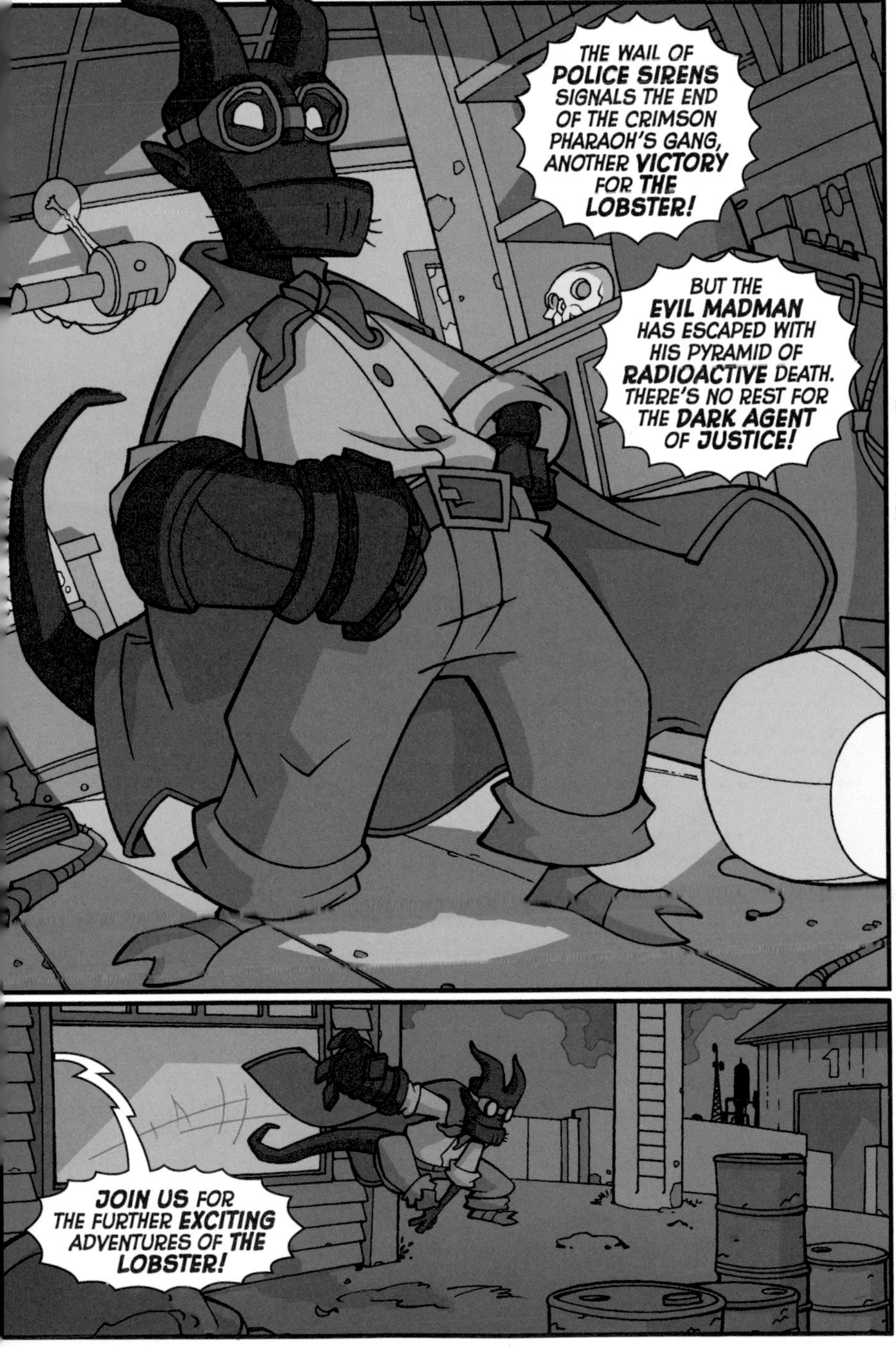
THE WAIL OF POLICE SIRENS SIGNALS THE END OF THE CRIMSON PHARAOH'S GANG, ANOTHER VICTORY FOR THE LOBSTER!
BUT THE EVIL MADMAN HAS ESCAPED WITH HIS PYRAMID OF RADIOACTIVE DEATH. THERE'S NO REST FOR THE DARK AGENT OF JUSTICE!
JOIN US FOR THE FURTHER EXCITING ADVENTURES OF THE LOBSTER!

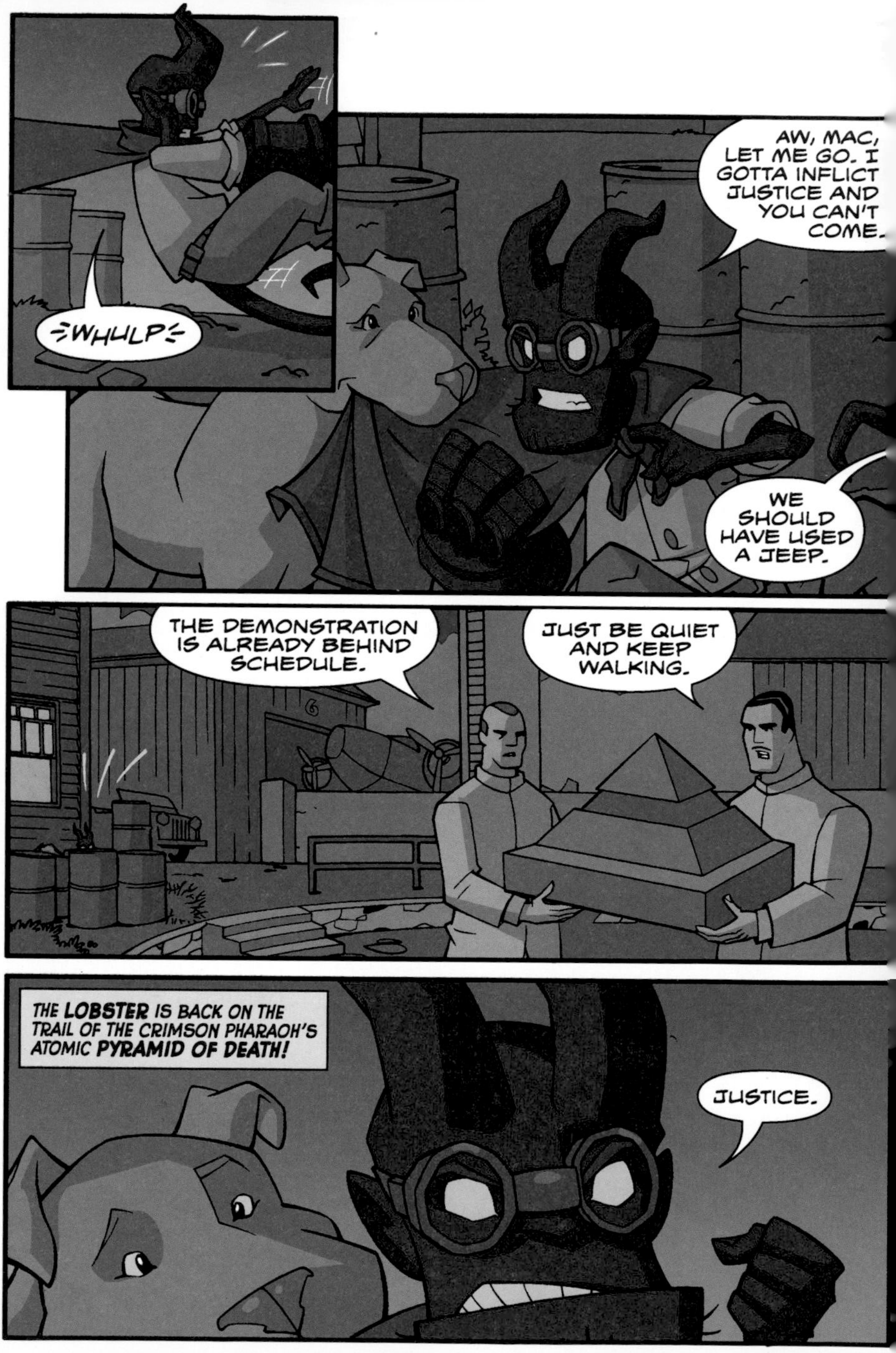
WHULP
AW, MAC, LET ME GO. I GOTTA INFLICT JUSTICE AND YOU CAN'T COME.
WE SHOULD HAVE USED A JEEP.
THE DEMONSTRATION IS ALREADY BEHIND SCHEDULE.
JUST BE QUIET AND KEEP WALKING.
THE LOBSTER IS BACK ON THE TRAIL OF THE CRIMSON PHARAOH'S ATOMIC PYRAMID OF DEATH!
JUSTICE.

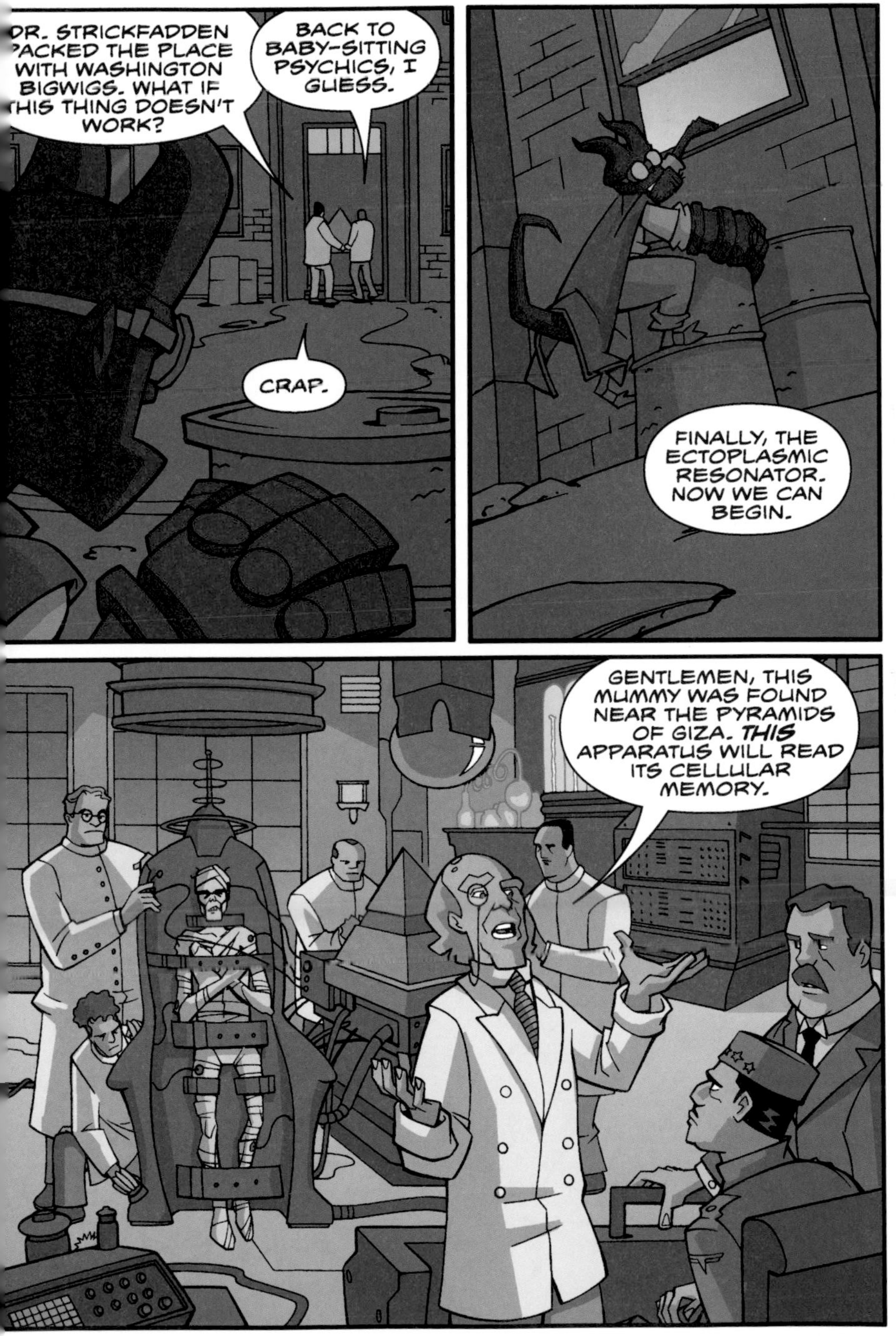
DR. STRICKFADDEN PACKED THE PLACE WITH WASHINGTON BIGWIGS. WHAT IF THIS THING DOESN'T WORK?
BACK TO BABY-SITTING PSYCHICS, I GUESS.
CRAP.
FINALLY, THE ECTOPLASMIC RESONATOR. NOW WE CAN BEGIN.
GENTLEMEN, THIS MUMMY WAS FOUND NEAR THE PYRAMIDS OF GIZA. *THIS* APPARATUS WILL READ ITS CELLULAR MEMORY.

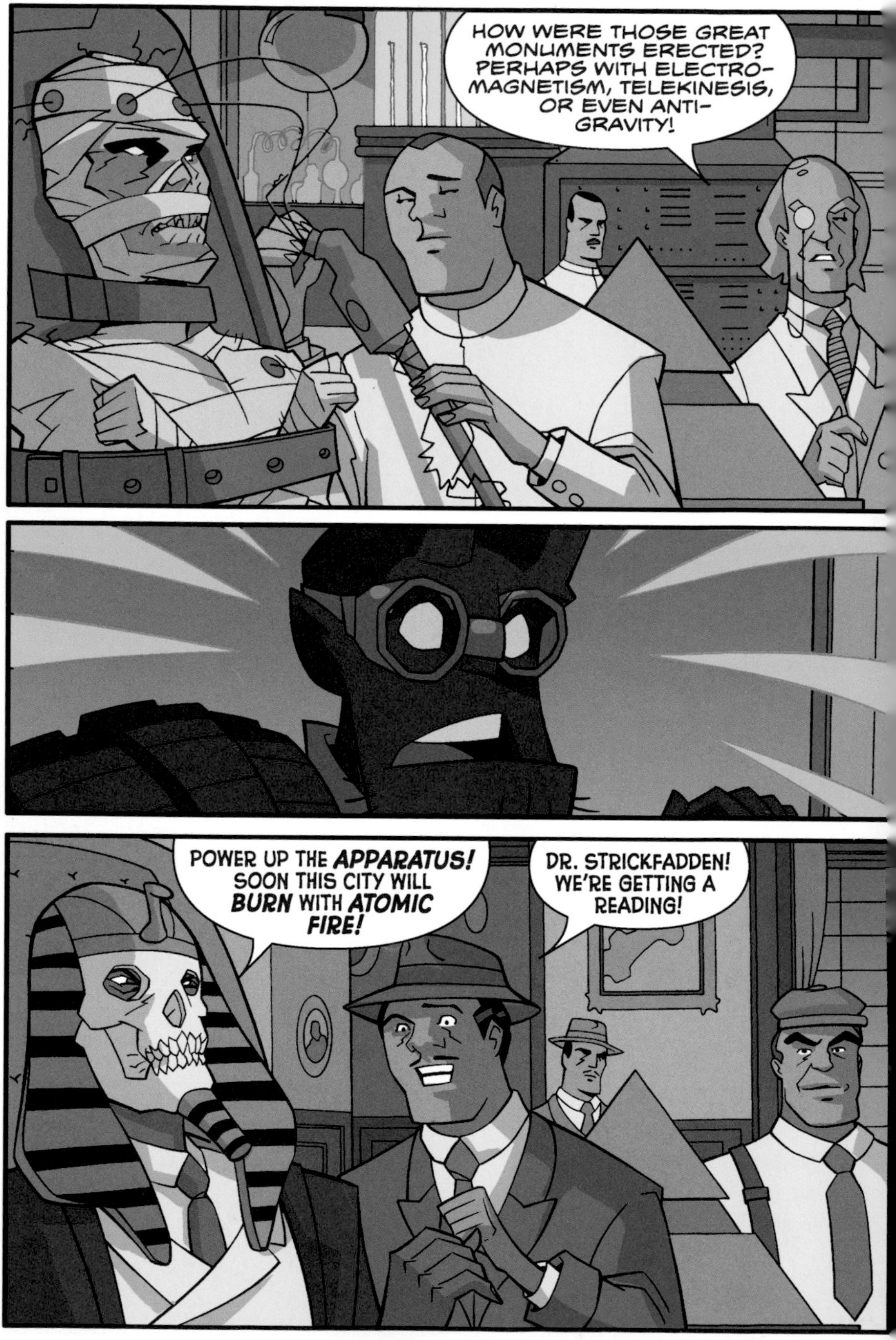
HOW WERE THOSE GREAT MONUMENTS ERECTED? PERHAPS WITH ELECTRO-MAGNETISM, TELEKINESIS, OR EVEN ANTI-GRAVITY!
POWER UP THE **APPARATUS!** SOON THIS CITY WILL **BURN** WITH **ATOMIC FIRE!**
DR. STRICKFADDEN! WE'RE GETTING A READING!

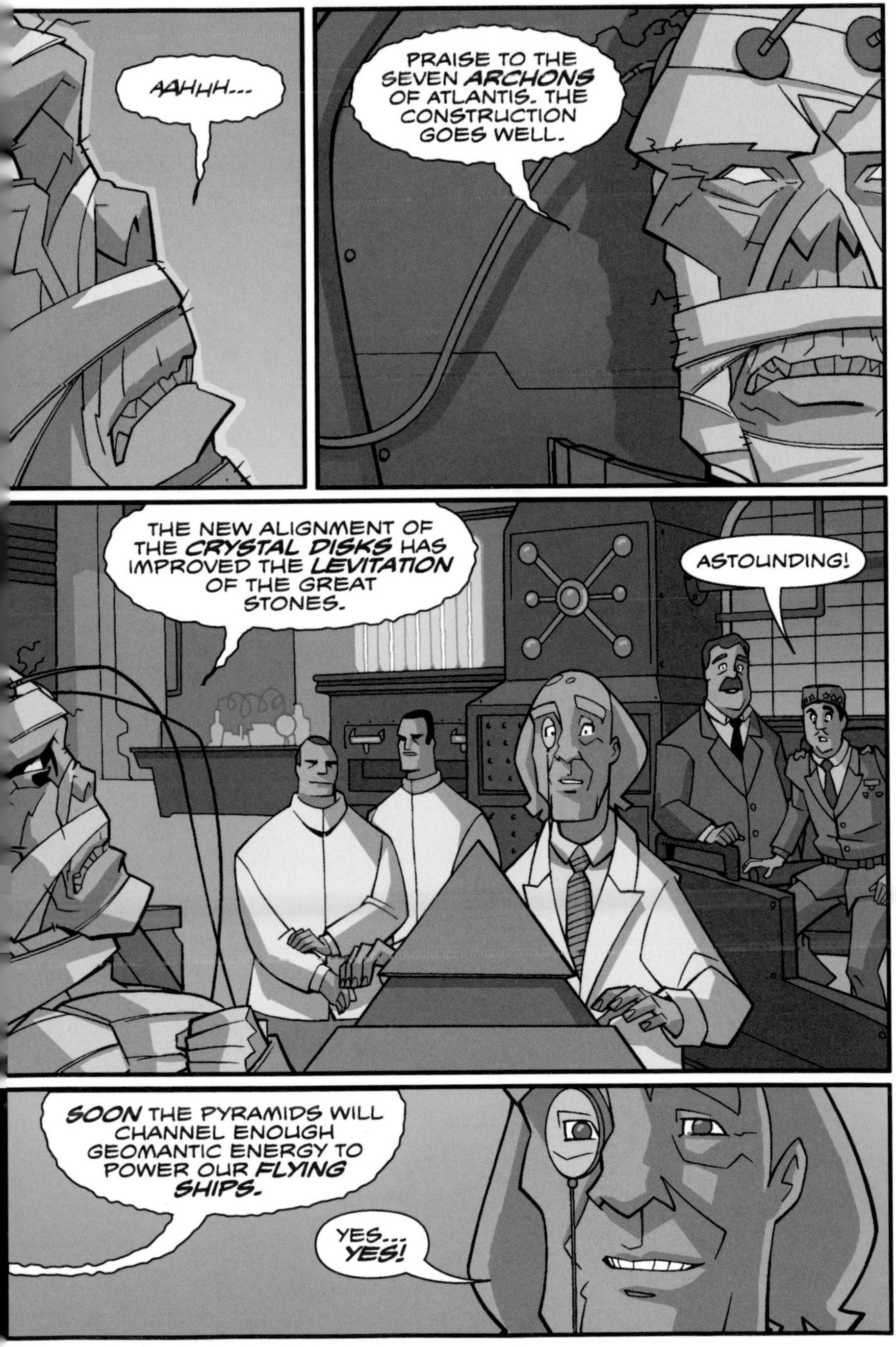
AAHHH...
PRAISE TO THE SEVEN ARCHONS OF ATLANTIS. THE CONSTRUCTION GOES WELL.
THE NEW ALIGNMENT OF THE CRYSTAL DISKS HAS IMPROVED THE LEVITATION OF THE GREAT STONES.
ASTOUNDING!
SOON THE PYRAMIDS WILL CHANNEL ENOUGH GEOMANTIC ENERGY TO POWER OUR FLYING SHIPS.
YES... YES!

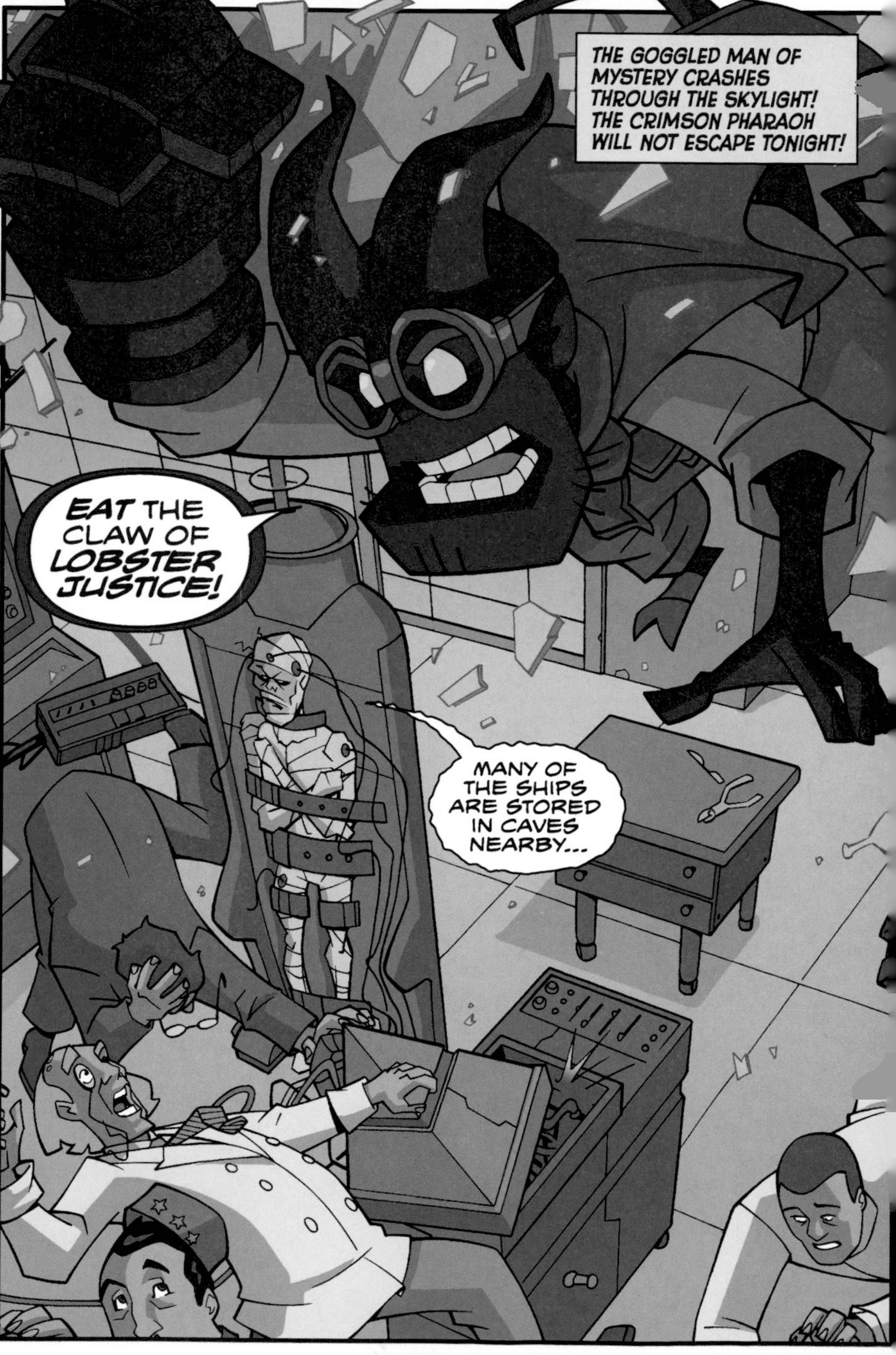

THE GOGGLED MAN OF MYSTERY CRASHES THROUGH THE SKYLIGHT! THE CRIMSON PHARAOH WILL NOT ESCAPE TONIGHT!
EAT THE CLAW OF LOBSTER JUSTICE!
MANY OF THE SHIPS ARE STORED IN CAVES NEARBY...

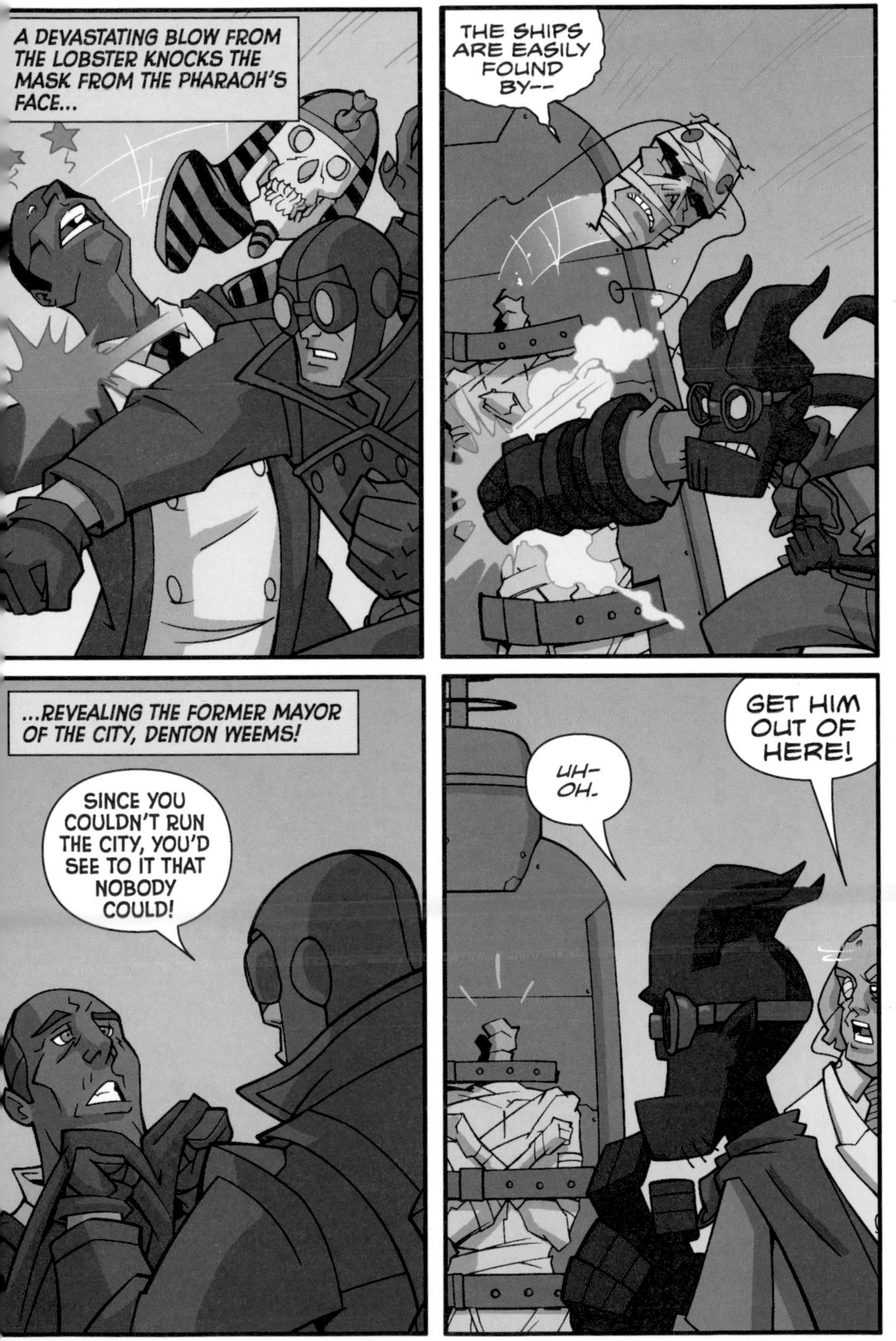
A DEVASTATING BLOW FROM THE LOBSTER KNOCKS THE MASK FROM THE PHARAOH'S FACE...
THE SHIPS ARE EASILY FOUND BY--
...REVEALING THE FORMER MAYOR OF THE CITY, DENTON WEEMS!
SINCE YOU COULDN'T RUN THE CITY, YOU'D SEE TO IT THAT NOBODY COULD!
UH-OH.
GET HIM OUT OF HERE!

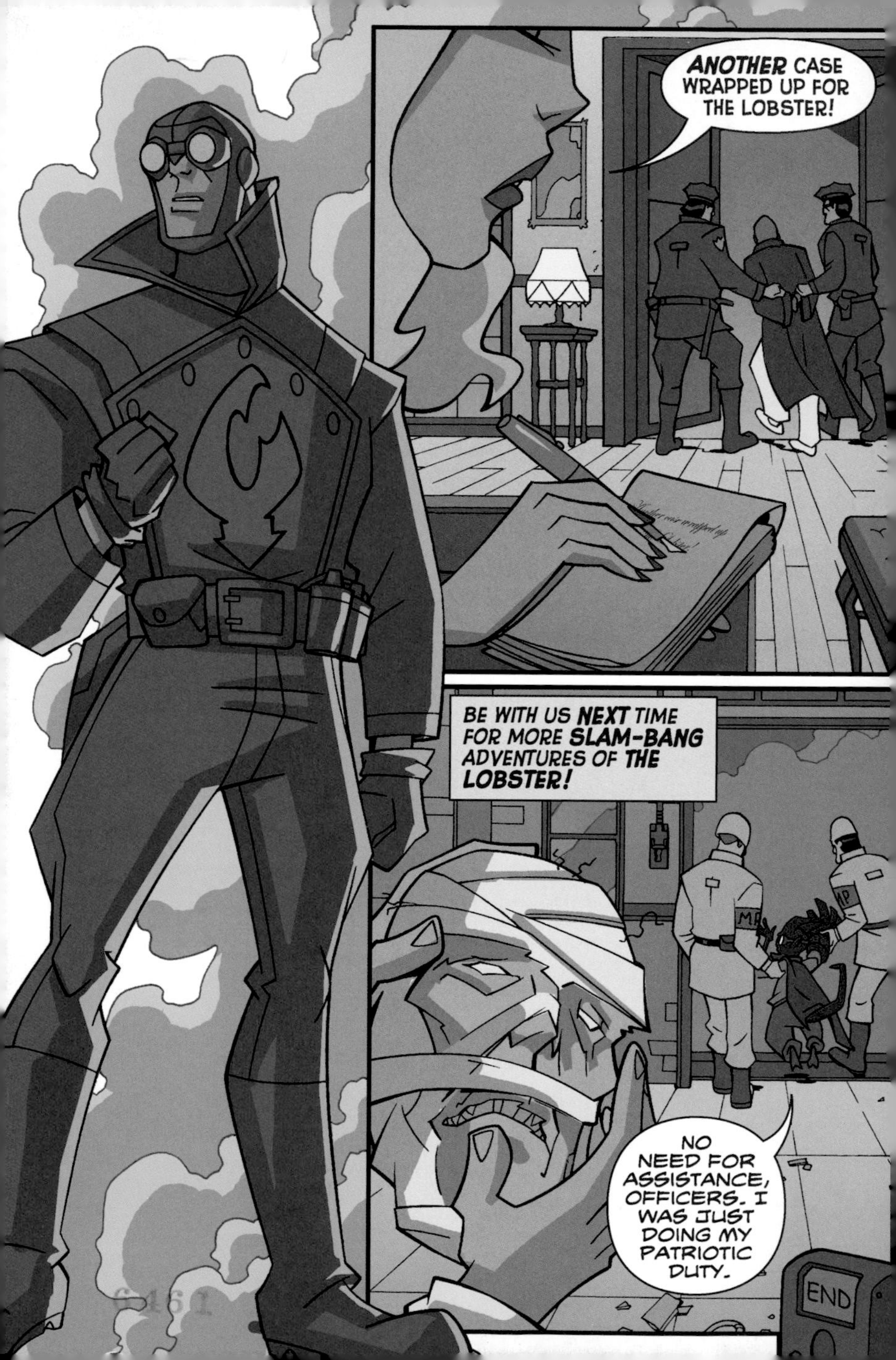
ANOTHER CASE WRAPPED UP FOR THE LOBSTER!
BE WITH US NEXT TIME FOR MORE SLAM-BANG ADVENTURES OF THE LOBSTER!
NO NEED FOR ASSISTANCE, OFFICERS. I WAS JUST DOING MY PATRIOTIC DUTY.
END

ALSO AVAILABLE FROM DARK HORSE

HELLBOY STATUE
10" tall, fully painted statue,
limited edition of 1200 pieces
$150.00

3 PIECE PVC SET
Hellboy, Abe Sapien, & Liz Sherman
$17.99

ABE SAPIEN STATUE
10" tall, fully painted statue,
limited edition of 1200 pieces
$150.00

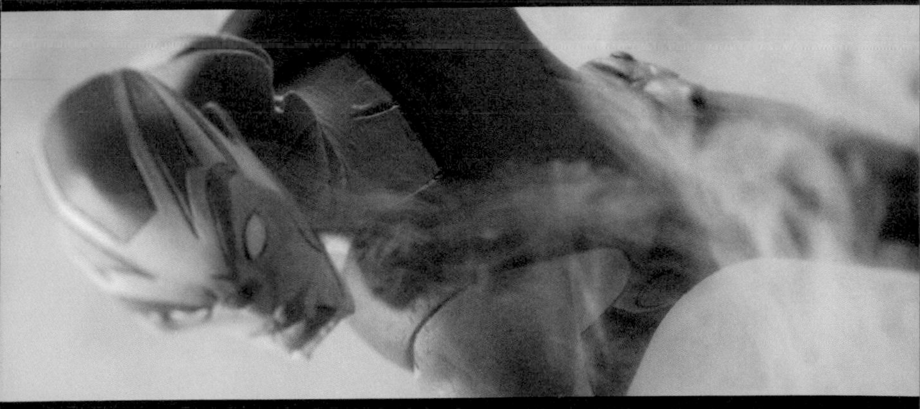

AVAILABLE AT YOUR LOCAL COMICS SHOP

To find a comics shop in your area, call 1-888-266-4226 For more information
or to order direct visit darkhorse.com or call 1-800-862-0053

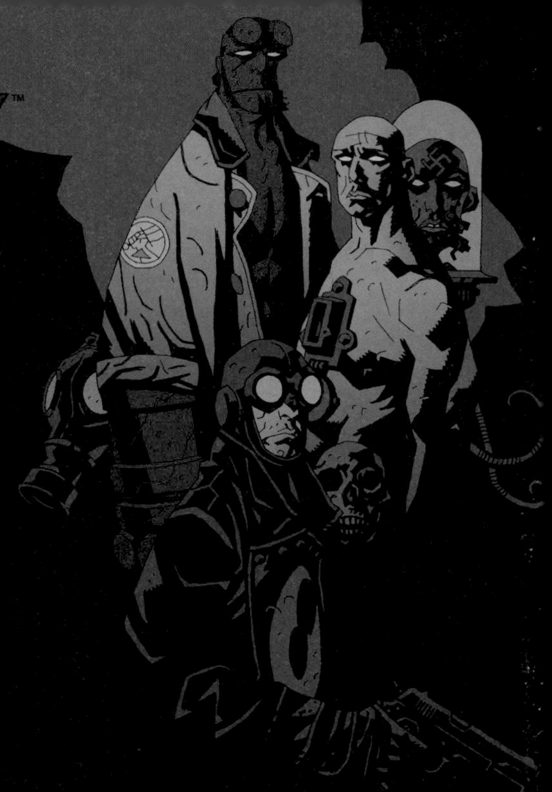